Rosa

A
Harlequin
Romance

OTHER
Harlequin Romances
by MARGARET WAY

Many of these titles are available at your local bookseller,
or through the Harlequin Reader Service.

For a free catalogue listing all available Harlequin Romances,
send your name and address to:

HARLEQUIN READER SERVICE,
M.P.O. Box 707, Niagara Falls, N.Y. 14302
Canadian address: Stratford, Ontario, Canada.

or use order coupon at back of book.

WIND RIVER

by

MARGARET WAY

HARLEQUIN BOOKS   TORONTO
WINNIPEG

Original hard cover edition published in 1973
by Mills & Boon Limited.

© Margaret Way 1973

SBN 373-01815-9

Harlequin edition published September 1974

*All the characters in this book have no existence outside the
imagination of the Author, and have no relation whatsoever to
anyone bearing the same name or names. They are not even
distantly inspired by any individual known or unknown to the
Author, and all the incidents are pure invention.*

The Harlequin trade mark, consisting of the word
HARLEQUIN and the portrayal of a Harlequin, is registered
in the United States Patent Office and in the Canada Trade
Marks Office.

CHAPTER I

FROM the top of the sand ridge, Faulkner could see the herd turning back on itself like the legendary Rainbow Snake, curving towards the west, milling, slowing up. Dead ahead lay the river; moody, unpredictable, the mighty Diamantina. It flowed across the Run, end to end, in time of flood, spreading out fifty miles and more; enormous, sprawling across the copper-hued spinifex plains, bringing up the sweet, fattening herbage that allowed the Channel Country to run its great herds.

This year the spring rains had failed and the crossing was no more than a silver sliver flanked by wide expanses of wind-blown sands. In another ten minutes, it would be churned up by thousands of pounding hooves, floating cloud castles on the air. The constant bellowing and lowing of the thirsty cattle reached Faulkner as a concerted roar. His big black stallion, Bodalla, tossed up its silver plume and he quieted it with one hand, his eyes screwed up against the shimmering heat haze, the quicksilver line of mirage. The sun was beating through his shirt like a throbbing pulse, all powerful, molten gold. He tilted his stetson rakishly over his eyes to shade them from the imperious sunlight. The herd was drawing on to the water now as though to a magnet. Rinka and some of the other boys were riding back and forth, flanking the mob leaders as they entered the water. If they got jammed up, there would be hell to pay. Faulkner moved his wide shoulders restlessly, almost visibly managing the operation, his demeanour not unlike that of a general reviewing his troops. That new jackeroo, Brady, had a long way to go before he was anything like a good stockman and his horse was too strong for him. With the same thought in mind, he saw Jake Rylance, his overseer, move down to the boy, issuing orders out of the side of his long, laconic mouth. Brady touched his hat respectfully and rode up ahead, pressing a steer back into the mob. Jake looked after him a moment, then stood up in the stirrups, looking back over the edge of the big herd as they milled around the crossing. With Jake around, things should progress well enough.

Faulkner wheeled the big stallion around and angled his way down the sand dune. On the other side, the open country ran on for miles – red, deep red, as big as the world itself. Ever since he could remember, he had been looking out over this same gigantic landscape, rampant with colour, aboriginal colours, the dry ochres, the burnt umbers, they used for their paintings, the rainbow-hued sandstone formations, the flame blue of the sky, the violets and indigos of the ranges; the whole, seamed by a network of water-bearing channels, like the lines on the face of Inkarta, the old medicine man.

The same, yet always new! Fresh in the memory. Hard to leave. Harder to forget, right through the long years at boarding school, then university, a few trips round the world, the accepted pattern with the old squatocracy. But he had clung to this, *Coorain*, his inner vision. The great holding that set him apart from most men, though it took him a long time to realise this, bred as he was to a big heritage. He took a deep breath of the dry, aromatic air, filled with a pride of possession, a man's great love for the land. Country like this made a man feel invincible. Country like this could lure a man to his death, lulled by the deceptive immobility of the featureless plains, the towering rose red bastions, the "sleeping giants", as his grandfather had dubbd them.

Sunset came in slowly and Faulkner rode on, enjoying it. This time of day the Big Country was alive with a potent magic. Deep pink and orange and gold played on the clouds banked high in the west, perceptibly resolving as the fingers of light lanced higher and higher like flame in a fireplace, shifting from orange and gold to deep red, a fiery glow that coloured his skin and his clothes with translucent effects. Only for a few moments would this fabulous light hold, then ... twilight. A purplish-blue haze over the desert. *Maratjoora*, the Simpson, the land of burning water, the mirage; a vast, awesome area of sand and gibber plains, claypans and more sand. Fifty thousand trackless square miles of quick death, variable winds and restless sands. An eerie place, a place of mystery and wild beauty after the rains and because of it, endless fascination. Somewhere out there, a lot of men had died. His father, one of them, a man who thought nothing was beyond his grasp – except crossing the Simpson even after the rains. The whole thing didn't bear thinking about, but that was the way his father had wanted it; a bizarre and untimely end, suicide in a way, although he had set out supremely confident of reaching the other side. Yet the brown man had survived from time immemorial with his miraculous affinity for his savage surroundings, the seemingly waterless wastes. But the brown man rarely passed on his secrets, bound up as they were with the tribal taboos, the sacred watering places.

Like no other place on the Continent, the Channel Country had a peculiarly aboriginal feel to it. The kiln-baked colours perhaps, or the legend of the great inland sea of pre-history, bordered by the favourite hunting grounds of a Stone Age people, starred with their sacred totemic sites, the fairy rings and mysterious peace paths. Which was, of course, why Greenwood wanted to come out here – Professor Lucas B. Greenwood, well known for his anthropological work among the *Pitjantat jara*, a recognised authority on the aborigines, their culture, their legends, the vast storybook of the Dreamtime, transmitted by word right down the ages, meticulously researched before it was too late. It was the rock paintings hidden away on Coorain that Greenwood was particularly interested in, precious as they were as a social commentary, the spiritual and artistic expression of a primitive people, cut off from the rest of the world, land locked in the great island continent, *Terra Australis*, the Great South Land, unknown and alien, with its unique wild life evolved and preserved through countless eons of isolation.

Spurring the black homewards, Faulkner frowned at

a passing thought, looking suddenly a very formidable man. A flock of green shell parrots ringed him round, but he scarcely saw them. Greenwood *and* party! His nephew and another assistant. He had given his permission so that was that! They were due to leave Bahl Bahla, his neighbour on the north-north-east border at eight o'clock the following morning, so they could be expected any time before sundown. Well, so long as they didn't bother anyone and got into no trouble themselves, they were welcome for the month or so they had requested to carry out their investigations.

Greenwood, a man of action, as well as a scholar, would know how to look after himself on any forays into the Big Country, but what of the other two? Faulkner had no time to nursemaid two bright-faced young graduates with no experience whatever of the Back Country. Running Coorain was enough for any man. He rode on, his thoughts given over to a long, cold beer, then a shower. The brolgas rose from the creek bed, rising and dipping with the wind, a ribbon of soft grey and bright red, and he was filled with an intense love for this land of his.

For miles, the scenery was of a strange, bizarre beauty. There was no sign of settlement, cultivation, grazing stock. Nothing but towering red cliffs with the white-boled ghost gums high up in the clefts, the vast dull gold spinifex plains, the silver glitter of waterhole and billabong, the dry windy bed of the river. Once a big red kangaroo with its blue flyer mate reared up in front of them, a hundred yards ahead, standing its ground, then plunged into the lignum. Overhead and before them a great flight of budgerigar, the phenomenon of the west, swooped in flock unison, the sun sheening their formation to blinding emerald.

Man against isolation! Perri thought, a shivery feeling starting at the base of her nape. She put up an involuntary hand and soothed the area of skin under the thick knot of pale hair, caught back for coolness. The whole country seemed to be still in its pristine state, hardly changed since the Dreamtime.

"It's rather awesome, isn't it?" she asked of no one in particular, breaking the two-mile silence. It was terribly hot inside the Land Rover and Mark turned on her with a faint flash of sarcasm.

"Wisdom from the young!" His eyes stayed on her with a snap of frustration; a cool blonde, illuminated skin, pale, pale hair, almost ash, grey eyes, faintly tilted, whispered with lilac, elegant bones, lightly covered, the whole adding up to something very tantalising, "don't-touch-me".

"Well, isn't it?" she persisted, a shade impatient of that fixed glance. "Honestly, Mark, I've never met such a one for staring. What's with you anyway?"

"I could hardly knock back the Prof just because I don't like his relatives," Mark said disdainfully, and turned his head away, resisting the mad impulse to catch her blonde head hard and kiss that lightly glossed mouth.

"Now, now!" Lucas Greenwood said mildly, only one part of his mind on the conversation, his veins quickening with excitement at what he might find on Coorain.

"One just doesn't realise how big the country is until one's exposed to all this," Perri said rather naïvely. "It seems so changeless, primeval. I can even see the Dream-time heroes walking among us handing out the laws of behaviour that all must obey or be punished by death!"

"You've a very fertile imagination, dear!" Mark said with open mockery, refusing to be influenced by her beauty.

"Can't *you* feel it, Mark?" Lucas Greenwood asked with sly humour, aware of Mark's interest in his brother's only child.

"No, I can't say I can. It's a bit grim, if you ask me – harsh and hostile. I'm beginning to feel like a square peg in a round hole!"

"Well, it makes for a little variety. A sound and capable team has been mobilised. Actually, I think Perri has the creative mind of the artist. Beauty takes many forms. All this affects me too and I'm not ashamed to admit it. This country has a queer kind of pull. It can even raise the short hairs on my neck. I can't explain it, and many old bushmen have told me the same. It's something felt, something primitive, I suppose. There were many bloody clashes around here in the old pioneering days. The white man with his sheep and cattle pushing on relentlessly into the Interior, the black man frightened and enraged, bitterly defending his sacred hunting grounds. Shocking reprisals were carried out on both sides during Queensland's Black War, you know, savage enough to rival anything in the saga of the American Wild West. The thing is, no white man has ever conceded an acre of ground to his primitive brother, and it's

11

been the same old story around the globe. What our fore-fathers accepted as natural and right and progressive was either abhorrent or completely incomprehensible to the tribes. They learnt at a brutal school and some of them surpassed their masters. These places don't lose their anguish with little more than a century to grass over the nameless graves. Perhaps it's the spirits of the unquiet dead. Who knows?" He said this in such a matter-of-fact way, without any trace of levity or sensationalism, that an atmosphere of grim actuality fell on them all.

"Bunkum!" Mark managed at last, shocked that the other half of him, like an enemy within, had given way to a sensation, macabre and without any scientific basis.

"Now that had a very rude ring!" Perri turned on him with sudden passion.

"I'm sorry!" Mark blinked at her vehemence. "No offence meant! But it does seem just so much rot!"

"Just as you like!" Greenwood said placidly. "But in fact it's a great deal more, my boy. Simple recognition of a fact. You don't need my say-so to believe it, young Durand. I've had it from a very eminent authority that the ghost of Francis Howard Greenway, the convict architect, still stalks the Hunter River Valley!"

Perri glanced over her shoulder, fractionally, at the now flushing and vaguely troubled Mark.

"Miserable?" she asked.

"Me?"

"Yes, you! Jumpy, too!" she concluded. "I pray there's not a ghost that haunts the Faulkner family. Don't worry, this trip is bound to take you out of yourself!"

"I don't want to be taken out of myself, thank you," Mark returned waspishly.

"Well then, it wasn't much use coming along, was it? You're one of those eggheads who combine a good brain with a total lack of imagination!"

"While you, my love, have it to excess! Such a godsend! But let me tell you, of all qualities, intelligence is the hardest to detect in a female. Men unquestionably have the fittest minds. Women should stick to something more in line with their mental powers!"

"What a fool you are!" Perri said with withering indifference.

"Children! children!" Lucas Greenwood shook his head, a big, handsome man, silver-haired, unfailingly tolerant, generous to a fault, yet withal a confirmed bachelor. "Supremely rational though I am, I still have an Achilles heel. I demand due respect from the young. Would you desist!"

"Sorry, Uncle Luke!" Perri smiled at him with an affection far exceeding the usual limits of relationship, at the same time resisting the notion to knock Mark's glasses off.

"I'm glad to see you do have a conscience. What about you, Mark?"

"May all your geese be swans!" Mark announced flippantly.

"The only snag is you two geese are my protegées!" the Professor retorted very smartly indeed.

"That's hardly *our* fault!" Mark looked grieved. Without his glasses he was young and very good-looking in a pale, Byronic fashion.

"I know. It's mine!" The Professor agreed. "The trick will be to get you to live up to your misbegotten degrees — if that's at all possible. Work like the devil to oblige me and you'll be allowed a little fun in your spare time. It was very good of Faulkner to allow us on the property. It wouldn't have been possible in his father's day. I should know. I got knocked back like an importunate tradesman at least twice!"

"But that's extremely unfair," Perri said heatedly. "Who do these people think they are? The cave drawings belong to all of us — a national heritage."

"The Faulkners might take that as treason," her uncle laughed.

"All I hope is, it doesn't add up to a lemon!" Mark observed from the depths of his pessimistic nature. "It makes you a bit envious, all the same. All this land! Four thousand square miles is a fair old step. No wonder at all they get a bit above themselves!"

"It's hardly *that*!" Luke Greenwood pointed out fairly, "but you're in the land of the cattle kings now, the seat of the landed aristocracy with all their influence and power. They're not like the rest of us and no one can pretend they are. I suppose when a man measures his property in the thousands of square miles, gives orders all his life, he develops a certain *style*, a certain manner — great self-possession, easily worn. That's been my overriding impression. It's something that comes with working these large land holdings. I've never noticed quite the same thing in their wealthy city counterparts. Perhaps it's the distant horizons, the space and the freedom. Whatever it is, it puts them markedly apart. Which

14

reminds me, Perri, if you want to take any pictures of the homestead, be careful to adopt the proper manner and beg permission!"

"Well, I hope to take a few!" she said a little defiantly. "Coorain made the first ten Historical Homesteads. From its pictures, it's a showplace – Colonial Georgian, with one of the finest private libraries in the country. I read up quite a bit about the family from the first John Gray Faulkner, who abducted his beautiful cousin who just happened to be betrothed to an earl at the time. The cousin, of course, was then scorned by the earl and locked up in the country while our hero or villain, make what you like of him, was transported to New South Wales as a 'voluntary exile' due entirely to the merciful intervention of his aristocratic mother. Needless to say he was received with great reverence by the bustling colony who expected him to pioneer the 'fashionable' life, but he confounded them all by becoming an Overlander and one of the most daring men of his day. Six years later with the beginnings of his vast fortune he sent a goodly sum Home and was rewarded by the reappearance of his cousin, and bride. They had seven children and ever since then there's been a John Gray Faulkner to grace every generation. Lovely, isn't it? A fitting climax. I wonder what today's John Gray looks like? Probably the old dashing image has misfired badly!"

"What's it to you, anyway?" Mark asked belligerently, always the one to hide his tenderest feelings beneath a cloak of aggression.

"I can dream, can't I?" Perri tilted her delicate black

15

brows provocatively.

"It wouldn't do you any good, dear," Mark pointed out with some relish. "The old squatocracy look to their own. The landed élite!"

"Breeding tells!" Perri agreed with wicked sarcasm. "I suppose we're actually honoured to be allowed on the old ancestral grounds."

"You could say that!" Luke Greenwood smiled rather dryly, "but if you promise not to look overawed, I won't! There's less emphasis on the old squatocracy these days. Even the élite have had to adapt to the changing pattern. Besides, they've had their tragedies in the early days like most of the big pioneering families. Even Sholto Faulkner, the father, never survived an unsuccessful attempt to cross the Simpson. From what I remember of the man, the only surprising thing is he *didn't*! A calculated risk after the rains. He was something of an adventurer, a super-optimist. His widow remarried a few years ago, as I recall."

Perri arched her throat and fanned it gently with a sheet of paper, oblivious of Mark's eyes with their dark intensity. "I remember now. An American, wasn't it? Connected with a Texas cattle syndicate. The *Women's Weekly* covered it. A small exclusive affair on Warrawee Downs, the home of Sir Hugh McDermott, the bride's father. The only reason I do remember it was because Sir Hugh presented the fashion awards this year on behalf of the Wool Board. A very distinguished-looking gentleman too, *and* his wife, the second one, I understand, is a good twenty years younger!"

"Lucky devil!" the Professor smiled. "There's no

doubt about them, they act like they own the earth!"

Mark leaned forward and tugged a shining strand of blonde hair. "Impressed?"

"*Very!*" Perri gave him a wayward smile that sent him right off balance. "Especially when I feel like indulging myself in a really violent love affair!"

Luke Greenwood looked rather dubiously at his niece. "Well, that gives me great comfort, I'm sure! What with the complete set of instructions I received from your mother!"

"If you want *my* advice, dear," Mark said confidentially, "I'd leave that sort of thing to those who know how to deal with it. In any case you're not going to find your grand passion here!"

"Why ever not?" she said blandly. "The present John Gray Faulkner is a bachelor, no less. I've checked. Besides, I'm terribly susceptible to the rich!"

Mark made a sound of utter censure. "You disgust me! In fact women as a whole disgust me!"

"That's all right, you've got to take them as they come," Perri smiled at him, her eyes shimmering maliciously. "We can't all be like you, my boy, twenty-four carat right through. But never mind, one day you're going to get what you deserve!"

"Oh, I say!" Mark sent her a narrowed glance, faintly bitter, but she ignored it and glanced out at the flying miles.

"This is rather like going round and round the mulberry bush, substitute spinifex!"

"I've just had a single battering thought myself," her uncle said mildly. "In this day and age could we be lost?"

"You're joking?" she looked at his heavy, handsome head.

"No, my dear, I'm not. The sombre unemotional fact is, we may or may not be lost. It's been in my mind for some minutes!"

This statement, delivered as it was in a dry, humorous voice, seemed so inimitably deft that Perri burst out laughing, further incensing Mark, who found it no laughing matter and said so very plainly. Lucas Greenwood only smiled, but Perri swung her head towards Mark, her tilted grey eyes sparkling like ice crystals.

"The transcendent virtue of coming from good British stock, *mon petit* Durand, is, we never lose our heads. Now if you sit back and be quiet we'll go to exquisite pains not to alarm you. Nervous, highly strung types like you just tick over like time-bombs till they die!"

"Perri! Perri!" her uncle intervened, "don't go and badger the boy about it, you're pretty volatile yourself! Please tell us, Mark, what you think. I've considerable respect for the quality of your judgement!"

Mark sat forward mollified, taking off his glasses and polishing them. "I distinctly recall saying about ten miles back, that wasn't the creek bed!"

"Oh, lord!" Perri breathed softly. "Must you always act the good boy of the class?"

Mark stared at her for a few moments in silence, with the curious brilliant intensity of the short-sighted. "You're a very strange girl, Perri. A puzzle I can't seem to solve!" The spotlight of the sun was right on her profile, emphasizing the clear, young perfection of her skin, the silver-gilt head. He couldn't seem to take his eyes off

18

her. He shook his head a little to clear it. "Everyone's entitled to his own judgement. I'm only trying to consider all aspects of the situation. The Professor did ask for my opinion. My honest verdict is . . . we're lost!" He paused with the air of someone who had given of their best in a difficult situation.

The Professor smiled sardonically. "Lost but still hopeful!"

"Man may be deluded by hope!" Mark observed moodily. "In the desert, at any rate!"

"Caution born of hard experience?" Greenwood turned his head for the first time, his own voice laced with sarcasm. Then he relented. "All right, Mark, that's fair enough and all in the strictest confidence!"

Mark flushed a bright pink. "The trouble with you, Prof, is your luck is so good you don't realise bad luck when you see it. These things usually go in threes as well!"

There was a small hushed silence and Perri threw out an irritable hand. "I'll have to keep an eye on you. You're going morbid!"

"God forbid! I'm a realist, that's all!" Mark protested angrily.

Greenwood wriggled in his seat, his bush shirt clinging damply to his back. He passed his hand across his eyes. "Ordinarily, children, I enjoy watching the friction of your two minds, but not now. Perri, get the map out. We'll retrace our steps to the last sandhill – take a few sightings, establish a few landmarks. Mark was right about the creek bed, let's face it. That's the trouble with this kind of country – it goes on and on for ever! Stretch-

19

ing away into infinity. The desert can be a friendly place, but it has some pretty harsh rules, calling for an understanding of certain fundamentals." He changed gear and swung the Land Rover around on the track.

The land lay vast. Copper-rust. Under the blazing vault of the sky they drove back the way they had come with a slight breeze from the south. Now the countryside took on a new, frightening dimension. A monotony of red ochre, rose pink, strange sandstone formations, splashed with yellow gold and the bright green of the minareechie. Not a cloud stood in the perfect blue density of the sky. There was no sound, only an unbelievable silence. No stirring of dust, no dust-devils but the ever-present shimmering magic of the mirage offering the cool and fragrant vision of an oasis in the heat-baked plains.

Perri dropped her eyes to the map. They couldn't possibly be lost. Better to regard it as an interesting theoretical manoeuvre. No longer was the Simpson rigidly inaccessible. Yet experiences and recent tragedies came to mind exerting their strong influence, fanned by the eerie atmosphere the desert itself evoked. The sand ridge loomed ahead, a formidable barrier, but the Land Rover was fitted to resist the toughest conditions with strong bars and plates across the front and plating underneath to protect it from stumps and rocky outcrops. As well they carried a forty-four-gallon drum of petrol, another of water and plenty of tools and appliances, and her uncle knew how to use them.

She cast a swift glance at his profile. He was the soul of resourcefulness and patient good humour, but in this heat he wouldn't have a young man's staying power. He looked a little paler, a little worn, or was that her imagination? The Simpson had established a grim reputation so that few people regarded it with less than a compelling fearfulness. It was unlikely that the Professor would underestimate its stark potential for danger. Unquestionably they were on its fringe.

Instead of skirting the sandhills as previously, Luke Greenwood now set the Land Rover at one, like an old warrior charger with all the confidence of a four-wheel drive and the roar of its powerful engine. To Perri's relief, it went sailing up the slope, struggled a little nearing the summit, thundered valiantly on, then came to rest at the top, cushioned by clumps of spinifex grass. If it wasn't frightening, what confronted them was breathtaking, as fantastic as it was eye-riveting. Glittering rose-pink sandhills ran in great parallel waves, a hundred feet high, built up by centuries of dominant wind action, pounding across the now barren inland sea of prehistory, hundreds of miles long, separated by perhaps a quarter of a mile or so. In the deep troughs the red ochre earth was studded with bright yellow clumps of spinifex spiky, low and quite spherical, some solid, some collapsible as straw castles. There was no sign of life, of any kind.

Perri found herself swallowing, some kind of primitive fear deeply embedded in her consciousness. This kind of country was pitiless, untenanted!

"Well, that little mistake cost us hours!" Greenwood observed, seemingly not greatly perturbed.

His attitude infused confidence into the two young

faces turned to him. "Do you know where we are, Uncle Luke?" Perri asked hopefully, disconcerted to find that her voice was slightly shaky.

He smiled and touched her cheek. "I know where we *nearly* were, my pet, but at least Coorain and Bahl Bahla have a line on our movements. Now let's have another look at that aerial survey map. There's a strong chance that if we cut across one or two sandhills we'll make up for lost time. There, put it down while I choose the best line for ourselves. Sand and tyres are natural enemies, but so far we've had little trouble. The thing will be to trundle over the ridges at the lowest point. Ah yes, I have it now!"

"How are we going to get out of *here*?" Mark enquired mock-casually.

"We'll just have to run down the other side and come up again," the Professor murmured, his mind on something else. "It's the devil's own job to keep the tyres in the tracks in reverse. Why, do *you* want to have a go?"

"Not on your life," Mark answered with alacrity, a good driver under conventional circumstances but without the high skill for the more serious headaches.

The descent was fast, simple, effortless, rather stomach-turning, but it took three running, whirring, roaring goes to re-skirt the sand ridge from its looser, steeper side. Down in the flat again they moved along quickly, almost buoyantly after their initial fright. By late afternoon the Professor was visibly tiring, making one of his lightning transitions from a big, handsome, silver-haired dynamo to his shadow self, a tired-out, much older man.

Without a word he surrendered the wheel to Mark and

they ploughed once more into one of the waterless channels that crossed their path, Mark seemingly bent on crossing as much territory as possible in the time available. On their fourth progressive sandhill, little more than fifty feet high, there was a complete absence of vegetational cover. The sand looked frighteningly loose, like the dark side of the moon where one could sink and be lost for ever.

Hunched up over the wheel, as if with actual physical effort, Mark ran the Land Rover forward. Twenty yards up the slope it came to a dismal halt. Mark swore unashamedly, wiped the sweat from his eyes, and reversed very slowly to the flat, then summoning up more power he charged the ridge again. This time they gained a few more feet before the engine fizzled out again. Down in the trough, the Professor and Perri got out, to give the lightened vehicle the best possible chance. Mark took off again to plough to a halt three-quarters of the way to the top, the tracks worn deep by the successive charges.

"We'll just have to try and push it!" Perri announced dejectedly, strands of pale hair falling around her heat flushed cheeks.

"Not in those tracks we won't!" The Professor cupped his hands and shouted up to Mark, who reversed with extreme caution down the loose sand. Nearing the bottom, the vehicle suddenly slewed grotesquely, one wheel whirring in unproductive effort, then it righted itself and came at a rush, narrowly missing the Professor. He jumped back with a great roar of pain, his arms locked around his upbent knee.

"Uncle Luke!" Perri's clear young voice echoed round

the empty sandhills, vibrant with fright. She could get the actual taste of it in her mouth, bitter and coppery. She ran across the intervening space with Mark scarcely a pace behind her. "How are you?"

"Bearing up!" Luke Greenwood collapsed on to the sand, gritting his teeth. "You ran over my foot, you young so-and-so. If I wasn't such a hero, I'd shriek!"

"Good God! I'm sorry!" Mark was gasping from his exertions. "I didn't do it to annoy you! I nearly turned the damned thing over, you know that. Anything broken, do you think?"

"The lot, I'd say," the Professor said tersely. "It's painful enough, I can tell you – badly bruised at any rate. Fortunately it was only the edge of the tyre and my foot was fairly deep in the sand, otherwise you'd have killed me. I feel sure of that. Things come in threes indeed! Persistence is your great weapon, my boy!"

"Oh, I feel frightful!" Perri burst out plaintively, her large eyes gleaming like grey satin. "I've lost every particle of my spirit of adventure and I'm hot and gritty as well!"

"Forgive me!" Mark implored her dramatically, intense about everything, feeling around for his glasses. They had come off somewhere!

"I suppose I'll have to!" she conceded rather uncharitably, "seeing we're likely to perish together. Can you stand up, Uncle Luke?"

"I *think* so!" Luke Greenwood rose gingerly to his feet with their combined assistance, putting his weight on his badly bruised toes. "Well, it's better than doing in the differential, I suppose. One can take heart from it!"

24

"Can we last out until help comes, that's the thing!" Mark grimaced with multiple sensations.

The Professor smiled wanly. "Give me some credit, you fool of a boy. I've come out of much worse situations than this one, even allowing for the kind of help that's available!"

"I don't think we'll have to come out of this one!" Perri shaded her eyes with her hand and looked up towards the sky, knowing an overwhelming sense of liberation. They all shaded their eyes and stared, their ears fine-tuned to a vibration that grew on the wind. It spoke help and an end to the physical distress Luke Greenwood must have been feeling.

"This puts us at a slight disadvantage if our host has to come looking for us," he observed wryly, looking rather pinched about the mouth

Perri looked at him with the sharpest concern. "Who the devil cares? It's the easiest thing in the world for these people to jump in planes and helicopters and that kind of thing. We haven't done anything to be ashamed of. It's a helicopter, by the way, and they've spotted us!" She ran a few feet up the sand dune and waved her hand, then, not satisfied with that, pulled the silk scarf from her nape and waved that as well Her hair spilled over her shoulder and fell down her back like a shaft of blonde silk. The angle of her taut, slender body, her slightly dishevelled appearance was having the oddest effect upon Mark.

"For God's sake come down!" he said, ludicrously tight-lipped. "There's no need to act the shipwrecked survivor!"

25

Perri jerked her head around with an air of shock, dusky sun spots standing in her cheeks.

"No harm in keeping our opponent off guard. A rousing welcome cuts a lot of ice with most men!"

"Yes, indeed!" her uncle smiled sourly. "If we all play it very casually, Faulkner may accept an appearance of strength for its reality. Failing that, I just could collapse. My foot's in the deuce of a mess!"

"You hear *that*!" Perri ran down the slope, a long-legged, grey-eyed gazelle, speaking sharply to Mark. "And you're so peculiarly heartless!"

Mark looked at the Professor apologetically, twitched a bit and begged to be excused for his behaviour. The Professor favoured him with a smile, not altogether humorous.

"That's all right, Mark. The great thing is to stick together!" He lifted his eyes to where the helicopter was buzzing overhead, orbiting the area, flying comparatively slowly and not high so that they could see the pilot manipulating the controls.

"They're setting down!" Greenwood said quietly. "Now for God's sake, let's confine ourselves to professional matters!"

"The whole damn business is like a military operation," Mark said with surprising bitterness.

"As exaggerated as ever!" Perri mocked him, literally gritting her teeth. "Don't worry your head about it, my boy, just let Uncle Luke do the talking!"

"It's one thing to be jerked out of a peaceful life and quite another to be dumped in the wilderness," Mark persisted, as much to annoy her. He shaded his eyes to watch the bright yellow helicopter hover for a few moments, then come down vertically to land quite gently on its skids some one hundred and fifty yards off. "Mission accomplished!"

They stayed together as a group while the door opened and a man jumped down from the cockpit.

"Yoho! yo bloody ho!" Mark breathed in Perri's ear, his young good-looking face twisted in wry amusement.

"Oh, do shut up!" she hissed, for some reason unspeakably disappointed, for the man who walked towards them was no man from a wonder world but a nice, ordinary, "concerned with their predicament", broad and stocky individual.

"Women – what fools they are!" Mark chortled, fully restored to good humour, "full of foolish fancies! A really violent love affair, ha ha!" He looked down at her profile, his black eyes sparkling. "It's a popular fallacy that because a man leads a remarkable life he must have a remarkable appearance. Our hero's straight from a horse opera!"

"I'd say you've got the wrong man!" Luke Greenwood smiled sardonically through his pain, his eyes on a taller, leaner figure that even at a distance had a slight touch of the infallible. The first man hesitated while the second caught up with him, then both men advanced on the party.

"S'truth!" Mark said for all of them, "that's Faulkner for sure!"

And so it was. John Gray Faulkner. Undisputed master of four thousand square miles. Arbiter of local dispute. Law dispenser. Local aristocrat. He looked it –

moved with a lithe, swinging vitality, spoke with the diabolical advantage of a voice that could equally well charm women as any high-strung filly in from the ranges.

"Professor Greenwood?" he asked pleasantly. "Faulkner. Jake Rylance, my overseer. I'm glad I played my hunch you might have struck trouble!"

In the heat of the sun, with the glittering red sand-dune as a backdrop, Perri's mind felt curiously disconnected, with the odd sensation she was floating above herself. It had to be the climate. Either that or she was over-reacting to a distractingly attractive voice, badly conscious of her less than perfect appearance, her flushed face and tangled hair, that extra button so carelessly undone on her shirt in a misguided effort to beat the heat.

Faulkner came on slightly ahead of the other man who had fallen back the required number of places, his purpose whole and undistracted, one hand out-thrust, unshakably self-assured, arrogant dark head on wide shoulders, eyes with the same intense brilliance of the desert sky, moving with vivid precision over all of them. Missing nothing!

All present and accounted for! Perri thought waspishly, with her shaken, too physical reaction. Her eyes were narrowed, almost defensively, her spine prickling like an irritable cat. It took no effort at all to see Faulkner had made a snap decision and found them all wanting. Socially acceptable perhaps, but *wanting* nevertheless.

Evidently Luke Greenwood was not of the same opinion. He went forward, smiling, dragging his foot very slightly, using his own brand of urban charm, making introductions, explaining away their series of mishaps as if they were no more than above the level of nuisance value. Perri willed herself to attention, smiling and shaking hands first with Jake Rylance, who regarded her with startled good humour, then Faulkner.

Her eyes met his briefly, her hand shivered away from that momentary hard contact. She tried to respond normally, fighting the certain notion that she was being pulled in a direction she didn't care to go. So here was a man's man who knew all about women! It was there in the eyes, alert and sensually alive, the curve of the long shapely mouth, that faint twist of devilment that challenged a woman twenty-four hours of the day. It took no effort at all to see the present John Gray Faulkner running off with a woman. Any number of women, for that matter. It scarcely needed to be his cousin.

Engrossed in her intensive, rather feline speculations, Perri quite missed his question. He looked down his straight nose at her, sharp, sardonic humour about his faintly uptilted mouth:

"The one contingency I wasn't prepared for! A *woman*!"

"I should hope so!" she shuddered fastidiously.

His glance struck hers with a glitter of laughter. "I don't know you well enough to follow that up. I'm only remarking that your uncle mentioned a 'young relative' in his letter. For some reason, which quite escapes me now, I took that to be a male!"

"Oh, I see!" she said tersely, straightening her shoulders.

"I appear to have wounded you?"

29

She caught her breath a little at his tone. "Not at all. It's just hard to explain some men's resistance to career women!"

He laughed outright. "Not at all! I'm all for them. Especially the good-looking ones!"

Perri turned away abruptly from the brilliance of those strange eyes, the faint laughter lines at the corner of that clearly defined mouth. She brought up a hand to brush her face in a voluntary effort to clear her mind. She felt irritable, edgy, if she would only admit it . . . excited! But she had come out here to work, not to teeter on the brink of disaster with a man like John Gray Faulkner. He looked just the man to have a violent affair with, if one only knew how to match him.

Mark, seeing her vaguely mutinous, troubled expression, narrowed his black eyes with graceless malice. Well, well, well! So that was how the land lay! John Gray Faulkner was a marvellous man — he had to admit it. Worth seeing on any terms. Bluer than blue eyes, a dark, dominating authority, polish and panache, but he had Perri all tied up in the knots of inexperience and antagonism. It sometimes happened like that, the only catch being, it could lead to almost anything. Mark moved back violently as Faulkner turned to Luke Greenwood with lithe, detached grace, bending to examine the older man's foot, his easy disturbing voice a fine blend of concern and a certain arrogant impatience. Mark forged up to where Perri was standing, grasping her fragile wrist with painful intensity so that she turned her brilliant, youthful face to him, slightly aghast.

"You're hurting me, laddie, believe it or not! Though

it makes a nice change from the usual ham-fisted adoration! "

"Bitch!" Mark murmured succinctly. "A truly blooded-minded female. Such sweetness is irresistible! Forgive the mad abandon, darling, but I could shriek at your reaction to Faulkner. Stalking about like an irritated cat with such delicate energy. But I'm right with you, old dear! What possible capacity for tenderness could a man like that have? Though I grant you his virtuoso ability in handling women. But you'd get hurt. *Hurt*, my silky-skinned silly innocent. Men like Faulkner aren't for beginners. You've got to try the lower orders first, gipsy's warning! "

"Oh, shut up, Mark," Perri said breathlessly. "You're crazy, I've said it all along! "

"I'm also, for my sins, a creature of very delicate perceptions," Mark pointed out truthfully. "No, don't lose interest, pretty one, underneath that feline antagonism I sense a certain glittery excitement. I know you pretty damned well, don't forget. Faulkner emphatically rates way above the average – in looks, in everything. That teak tan is terrific. Could it be fairness recognizing darkness? The two of you together make an almighty impact! "

Perri's eyes were unchanging, a clear, shimmery grey. She spoke sharply, but she meant to be sharp. Mark was undoubtedly trying to goad her.

"I've had to accept the fact, Mark, that you've a pretty primitive sense of humour! "

"Accept what you like! " he chopped her off smartly, "but don't let it recoil on your head. Better the devil you know than Faulkner you don't!"

The sun lit Perri's hair so that it fell like a silver quill over her shoulder. "Oh, don't be a fool, Mark. I've got all the excitement I can use!"

"Have it your own way, sweetheart!" Mark's eyes on hers were black and unreadable. "But there's a touch of fear and fascination in the way you look at Faulkner."

"Wonderful!" Perri said lightly, though it cost her an effort. "You've just made a unique contribution to the sum total of human wisdom. We can expect big things from you, Mark. It just so happens Mr. Faulkner leaves me cold!"

"*That's* plain to see!" Mark went on in a deceptively soft voice. "I just hope I'll be allowed to compete!" The expression in his eyes deepened. "If I had any sense at all I'd remove you from his influence as soon as possible. I've the sickening notion that you'd succumb all too easily."

"Why not?" Perri rejoined flippantly, brushing her tongue over her top lip. "I imagine he's well used to that. So you'd better get cracking on a plan, hadn't you?"

Mark didn't look at her but gave a funny twisted little grin. "Let the flames of the fire touch me! Who said that? I could have even made it up myself. At any rate it's what you'd expect of a female with your eyes and mouth!" He shook his head violently, rousing himself from what he termed to himself as a "lunatic state" compounded of the heat, his fatigue and the shocking premonition that John Gray Faulkner was already a major new dimension in Perri's young life.

"I'm damned if he is!" he exploded suddenly, and

swung about watching Perri rub the marks on her wrist. "Don't think I enjoy doing this, angel, but it's all for the good of your soul. Many could have been saved with a timely warning!"

"Fiddlesticks! The only flaw being you've built on a mistake!" Perri said, sweetly reasonable.

"I was brought up to distrust girls like you!" Mark said soberly, such a look of longing on his face that Perri, charmingly and generously, encircled his shoulders in an effort to comfort him, drawing a finger down his cheek.

"Now don't be a bigger goat than you have to be! You and I are out here to work, and I promise not to let the team down. I shan't! I shan't!"

But Mark was not to be comforted, his eyes, encountering Gray Faulkner's bluer than blue gaze, amused, slightly cynical, supremely adult. He pulled away from Perri in a frenzy of rejection.

"Would you be good enough not to kid yourself!" he hissed at her, his breath stirring the silver-gilt tendrils that wisped on to her heat-flushed cheeks, then he made straight down the track to where the others were waiting, with varying degrees of interest on their faces. Perri followed, enjoying the arrogant satisfaction of evading a vivid blue gaze, but the strange, so familiar voice spoke, giving her a moment of bitter delight.

"When you're ready, Miss Greenwood, Jake will take you and your uncle back to Coorain. That foot must be giving him a great deal of pain. Nothing broken so far as I can detect, but he should be off it as soon as possible."

"And what about the Land Rover?" she asked in a

curious, vaguely censorious tone.

"Durand and I will bring it in," he returned suavely, giving Mark a nonchalant glance. "Don't worry, we don't intend to abandon it!"

"That's very good of you, Faulkner." Luke Greenwood turned his heavy leonine head, giving the younger man a look of respect that made Perri uneasy. Gray Faulkner had his victories much too easy.

"Not at all!" the dark, easy voice went on. "It was very good of you to take all the blame for the mishap!"

"When the classic excuse would have been to blame *me*, the weakest link," Perri burst out with devastating frankness, something quite unique in her experience seizing her impulses.

Blue eyes, slightly hooded, were directly on her so that inexplicably her whole body tingled. The shapely mouth curled.

"You've a very decisive air about you, Miss Greenwood, as well as being extremely pleasing to the eye."

She turned her head swiftly to look up at him, feeling hot and discomfited, at a definite disadvantage. "That's true enough!"

He laughed outright and she bit her lip, lowering her lashes quickly over her sparkling eyes, then caught her uncle's faint, all-male grin. "If it's all the same with you, Uncle Luke, I'll come back in the jeep. Challenge and Adventure, that's my theme. I don't want to do it the easy way!"

Gray Faulkner looked down at her shining, pale head, his dark face faintly intrigued.

"Well, whether that's good or bad is hard to say, but

it's definitely worth while to meet a woman so undeniably single track!"

"Thank you, Mr. Faulkner!" she said bluntly, because that was all she could manage. "I'm coming Please?"

"Why not?" Thick sooty black lashes hid his eyes. "There's no reason to let you off so easily, besides I've fallen behind with all the city gossip! I might mention that we won't make it by nightfall, which means we'll have to camp out." He trained on her such a look of merciless humour that instantly she stiffened her spine. "The glamour worn off?" he inquired politely.

She drew a little breath, seeing his dark head outlined against the brilliant desert sky. "Not at all. Merely strengthened with two strong men to look after me!"

"Half your luck!" Mark commented briefly, his black eyes rapier sharp, "but surely the Prof needs you. One would have thought . . ."

"Yes, of course!" Instantly Perri was brought back to reality, young and contrite.

"Don't be silly, my dear." Luke Greenwood had to smile. "You have your adventure by all means. You're young enough to count it one. I'm well used to looking after myself, though one wouldn't think so right at this moment!"

"I can see I'll have to let you in on some of my more spectacular miscalculations," Gray Faulkner said in an easy drawl, grasping the older man's arm and speaking across the thick silver head to his overseer. "Right, Jake, let's get the Professor back to the helicopter. You know the score. We'll set out at first light, always supposing we can rouse our intrepid lady explorer!"

35

Perri drew in a faint whistling breath and Jake Rylance smiled knowingly into her exasperated face, the entrancing line of colour that rose under her clear skin and mantled its matt creamy texture. "It never does to bite, Miss Greenwood. Take it from one who knows!"

"The way I see it, Mr. Rylance, one couldn't very well help it. But I agree, dignity's the thing!"

"And *you* much too young for it, but that's scarcely your fault!" Gray Faulkner spared her an amused, narrowed glance. She sustained it as best she could. Jewelled eyes in a darkly arrogant face, charm so palpable it was hard and disturbing, frightening almost. She kept her chin tilted, her delicate brows arched, but speech wouldn't come. She was still at a loss, knowing him a man who would always be those few telling jumps ahead. Madness seemed to be taking possession of all her senses, she thought dazedly, and lifted one white uncertain hand to shade her tilted grey eyes.

He gave a brief laugh looking down at her and she could see it was *at* her. Then he moved quickly, with that swinging dark vitality she had come so easily to recognise, standing at Luke Greenwood's shoulder. "Right-ho, Professor let's go. Miss Greenwood, your last chance?" He slanted a quizzical gleam over his shoulder.

Beside her Perri could feel Mark's eyes boring into her like gimlets. "I'll see you back at Coorain, Uncle Luke," she said, keeping her attention on his face, and crossed to kiss his proffered cheek.

"You *are* on Coorain, honey," Gray Faulkner pointed out idly, looking down his straight nose at her. Then she was left staring at the broad line of his back, that extra-

36

ordinary miasma of relaxed power. It was quite something to see him take the necessary steps to get Luke Greenwood into the helicopter with the minimum amount of discomfort. Once done, he got well back, moving slowly towards Perri and Mark as the rotor spun into action.

The helicopter lifted vertically in little scurries of red dust devils and they all lifted their arms automatically to wave it off. Across from them Gray Faulkner dropped a negligent hand to retilt his stetson, getting the benefit of the slight breeze through his dark hair. Perri watched him with some concentration. There was an air about him that she had never yet encountered.

"Five will get you ten!" Mark hissed in her ear, in a malicious cascade of false laughter. "Even if you could get him, sweetie, he's poison. The dilemma is plain!"

She spun on him in a fury, irritated beyond measure with his line of attack, its bitter kernel of truth. "Lay off me will you, stupid, and stop acting like you've bumbled across the latest issue of *True Confessions*. You're raving mad!"

"Every day in every way we learn something," Mark chanted, sadly off-key, regarding her heightened beauty, her increased aura of femininity as though it fed on some bright flame. "You're learning about someone – *yourself*. But there's one risk you ought to consider. Gray Faulkner is trouble, double trouble. He's too worldly by far and you're just a green kid. I doubt if a real woman could face the situation any too calmly. Camp out?" he snorted. "You beauty, all right! Dream lover, put your arms around me!"

Perri almost flung herself from him. "Whose temper are you trying to lose?" she inquired with acid humour, fighting the odd, rootless excitement that was riding her down, angered and unsettled by the line Mark had taken. This harping on an odd, unexpected, cross-threaded antagonism/attraction knowing in her heart that in some unfathomable fashion, Mark held the key to the truth. The senses were traitorous with passion the lord of them. Gray Faulkner was at once and forever the kind of man who would shock any woman out of her apathy. A bitter pill, that; but she wouldn't be the first to come to terms with it. Women were the romantics, men the hard-headed realists. To gain any other notion was to go flat on one's face.

"Oh, come on down to the jeep," she said irritably, "seeing you don't want to apologise for your outrageous behaviour. I couldn't bear any more of Mr. Faulkner's speculative glances, and here he comes now!"

"*Mr*. Faulkner?" Mark said witheringly. "Can't you figure out something better than that?" He began to whistle, then blew out his cheeks. "He even makes *me* feel like an old, done man. Rakish lover, I bet. Cattle baron. Class. How the hell does he *move* like that? I must try it. Controlling the situation with only half his mind, the other half on far more important matters. But he's noticed you, kiddo. Funny, that. It must be something innate – recognition. Twin souls and all that."

For a moment Perri was nonplussed by his intensity, his seeming bent on making mountains out of molehills, then, because she was fond of him, she burst out laughing and in a minute Mark joined in, holding out a frail

38

sort of olive branch between them.

"Now please don't embarrass me with any more of this nonsense," she said in a small girl coaxing tone. "It's unnatural!"

"It's ridiculously *sudden*!" Mark countered belligerently, excessively irritated by her tumbled hair, the slight alluring curve of her breast. "The question is, will there be an end to this madness?"

For some reason, not even known to herself, Perri blushed scarlet, then surged on ahead, her head high, her eyes shimmering like the sun on a lake. Gray Faulkner, watching her approach, addressed her thoughtfully, "So anxious to go?"

"You'll have the devil's own dance getting the Land Rover mobile," she countered for want of something better to say.

White teeth flashed, a slash of light out of dark. "Watch me. It's all done with wheels and a little knowhow." He turned fractionally, a tall, very lean man, but powerfully built, then with uncanny thought sense looked searchingly into her face. "Settle down, for Pete's sake, though I can see the boy-friend has been working pretty damned hard to make sure you register all the appropriate emotions." His bluer than blue gaze sharpened with irony. "What were you arguing about, in any case?"

"It would be a shade indiscreet to say," she murmured rather helplessly, "particularly with you right there in front of me!"

He side-stepped her neatly, laughing in his throat. "Like that?" A little silence fell between them. He was looking directly into her eyes, holding them for a moment. They seemed cool, faintly cynical, the iris dense with colour, a little amused. The white teeth flashed again. Obviously something had struck him as humorous, but he wasn't prepared to share it. He flickered a backward glance over Mark's averted, determinedly indifferent face. "Stay put over there with the boy-friend and no helpful suggestions. I just know you're the kind of female that makes them."

"We could, if you like . . ." she began earnestly.

"Over there!"

"Yes, sir!" she said smartly, and smiled, unexpectedly amused by the change in his tone. It just didn't seem possible to have so many attractive inflections in the one voice. Right at the moment he was the cattle baron with little time to spare for the weaker sex. Perri did what she was told, crossing back to Mark, her eyes on the tracks sunk deep in the sand. Mark grunted, without speaking to her, remembering his own successive charges, the thundering engine and the phenomenal petrol consumption, but Faulkner just kept on walking, opening the door of the Land Rover and slipping into the driving seat.

He turned the vehicle about and incredibly, to Perri's way of thinking, began to reverse up the tracks, somehow managing to keep the wheels in the tracks. The Land Rover made it to a point hitherto unconquered, then fizzled out, apparently defeating the seemingly unbeatable Faulkner. Mark gave a small insulting grin, a kind of "sand, the great leveller", but Faulkner slammed out of the vehicle, moving across the sandy ridge with sure purpose, stark on the brilliant skyline. He seized on what few gidgee branches he could find, throwing them down in the deep tracks, obviously in an effort to gain traction, at one and compatible with the rugged nature of his surroundings. On the fourth successive try with the engine roaring mightily he made it to the top and it was all over.

Perri found herself cheering, at the same time visualising how long it was going to take them to vault the successive sand ridges from their looser, steeper side. But that was Faulkner's job. In some ways it was truly wonderful to be a man. She turned to Mark, her eyes dancing in open relief, and even Mark couldn't quite conceal patently similar feelings, though he tried his hardest.

"Hail the conquering hero!" he murmured with a grotesque grimace. "Now here we have a man who knows how to get things done!"

"Practice, my lad!" Perri said buoyantly. "But what's that to us? Come on, let's go. Mr. Faulkner awaits us. At a guess I'd say twiddling his thumbs wouldn't be one of his more notable characteristics."

"No, but what the others are, we'll sure as hell find out!" Mark said prophetically, and began to ascend the flaming lines of the sandhill with the sky a fiery violet-blue streak. At the summit Faulkner's dark head and long lithe body were thrown up in the brilliant glare, shimmering in the mirage so that even to Mark, the whole scene, man and his savage environment possessed a wild grandeur, wholly in keeping with the giant landscape.

One thing was certain, he thought mournfully, and it only added to his general feeling of emotional pandemonium – there wasn't going to be one monotonous moment on Coorain!

CHAPTER II

MOONLIGHT in the desert, soundless in its peace, the stars blazing out of the soft, purple night Perri rested lazily against the side of a boulder, lost in a kind of dreamy introspection, an equal mixture of physical exhaustion and romanticism, yet she didn't feel in the least like going to sleep, drawn into a web of relaxed dreaming. There was no urgency now. The long day was over, evidently with a devastating toll, for only a few feet away Mark was already fast asleep, mercifully not snoring, but "sun-scorched, body aching, eyes glazed by the heat and mirage" – the whole bit, she thought to herself, a smile breaking around the corners of her sensitive sensuous mouth. She stretched her slender body, savouring the night, on her face a languorous, captive expression.

They were well into Coorain and Gray Faulkner knew every inch of every square mile of it. She hadn't a worry in the world. In the centre of the small clearing, the glowing coals of the camp fire threw a beacon of harmony and security into the night, heavily scented with the wild boronia, the night-blossoming desert lilies, a host of narcotic shrubs. Perri shifted her gaze to the enchanted night. Sky Country! Brilliant in the rarefied air. It spoke great magic to her; the Milky Way a shimmer of luminous light, a procession of diamond clusters, unutterably lovely. No wonder at all that the ancient people had worshipped the Sky People as deities.

Some kind of bird, perhaps a night hawk, whistled from the deep shadows where the wind soughed through the bauhinias, the eucalypts, the shining pretty minareechie. There was a magic about the Outback that had to be experienced to be believed, a kind of giant step into the Dreamtime, an atmosphere that was almost unreal, with the totem and spirit creatures at rest in the sandstone hills. The small dead leaves in the soft belt of mulga scrub rustled and something scurried over her foot. It did odd things to the nape of her neck and her heart. She quivered and jumped, stifling a little cry which attracted the attention of Gray Faulkner as he walked into the circle of light.

"What's up?" He deposited an armload of dry kindling and turned swiftly to her, alert on the instant exaggeratedly tall, the firelight caught in his brilliant eyes.

"I really don't know!" she jerked out. "Bad magic perhaps, or some little debil-debil slithered over my foot!"

His ghost of a laugh mocked her. "I can't understand that at all. Sure it isn't the nervous strain of it all?"

She glanced downwards a little fearfully. "Oh, come now, Mr. Faulkner, I'm a big girl now. I tell you something took a short cut over my toes!" Almost at the same moment she was confronted by a pair of gleaming little eyes staring balefully, a glazed red.

"Oh, lord!" she moved like a blue streak, clutching out

43

for Gray Faulkner as though he alone could save her from the brink of disaster.

Quick fingers closed over her wrist and pulled her up to him, stirring her blood and making her pulses quicken. "Keep your distance, but not tonight!" he jeered lightly. "Jirridilli, the sand lizard, a force to be reckoned with out here!" His laugh touched her cheek. Her reaction was all physical, uncaring, an element innate in her temperament. She spun her head and her hair fanned out, hazing his shoulder.

He brushed it away with a lazy finger. "That hair! Enough to wreck a man!"

"I'm sorry, I made rather a fool of myself!"

"That's what I like about you," he countered with bold impudence. "You *talk* big! Shall we do it again? We might need more practice!"

Deliberately Perri moved towards the firelight, her spine prickling, steered from the quick sand of attraction to antagonism. "I'll say this for you, Mr. Faulkner, your self-assurance is unshakeable."

"*And* it's not from pure chance!"

"Have it your own way!" she said rather tersely over her shoulder.

"As usual!"

The bantering voice, the underlying amusement, that dark glitter of devilry made her physically breathless. "Oh, go to the devil!" she said as if she had come to a momentous decision.

His voice slowed to a drawl. "Courtesy will get you nowhere, Miss Greenwood! Now what about turning in? It's been a long day at that!"

She lifted her head, her eyes shimmering, feeling resistance was clearly out of place. "The voice of authority, I take it. You think a lot, obviously, of controlling people!"

"Difficult, isn't it? Don't think I don't feel for you!" He smiled at her in an attractive, calculating fashion. "How about it? Come quietly or you'll be a liability in the morning. The boy-friend flaked out a good hour ago. You'd do well to follow his example!"

"Yes, of course!" she said stiffly, delicately outraged at being so dismissed. Her expression became unutterably aloof.

He caught the point of her shoulder as she went to pass him, tilting her head to him. "Now then! That's very unmannerly!"

"What is?" She shook her pale head, a little dismayed.

"What you're thinking. It will go much easier for you if we're friends. Besides, surely in this world we must trust somebody!"

Her faintly hostile face, extravagantly feminine, was upturned to him. "I'm not with you at all!"

"Oh yes, you are!" he pointed out with certainty. "All the way!"

She shrugged her shoulder free of him, avoiding his eyes with their vivid insinuation. "I knew it all along – a man of iron perception!"

"Now what piece of feminine logic have we tumbled across?" His glance slid over her. "Why quiver like that? My motives are of the most chaste!"

His voice seemed to be part of the night, with the

night's soft magic. She was breathless all of a sudden, nervous enough to back away.

He shook his head. "Not a clash of wills? I wonder who'll win?"

"No contest at all, Mr. Faulkner!" she said, dampening his lively interest. "I've just decided I don't feel like a fight!"

"Wise girl!" he said agreeably, increasing her exasperation. The moonlight fell on her hair, a pale glittering ash-gold.

"Physical attraction," he said idly. "It brings its penalties as well as its rewards! Monstrous, of course, but there you are!"

"Which reminds me," she broke in smoothly, "I'm as utterly fatalistic as you are. There's really no need to point such things out. I've long since decided against all possible rewards!"

"*You've* decided!" he laughed beneath his breath. "Haven't you learnt a man goes passionately after what he does not possess!"

For a moment no comeback occurred to her, then she said lightly:

"It must be the effect of the sun on my head. I feel a little mad!"

"That's not difficult to understand. What better reason to call it a night, entrancing as this conversation is. Come on, play your cards right and I'll even lend you a blanket!"

"I'm overcome!" Sarcasm showed in her opalescent eyes.

He smiled in a leisurely way. "For no good reason,

ma'am! Let there be no reticence between us. I believe in sharing things as a Christian should!"

Perri lowered her lashes, unable to resist clicking her tongue. He unnerved her so deftly.

"What a lot of traps you've fallen into today!" he observed nonchalantly, then moved with a soft elegance, opening out her sleeping bag, adjusting it neatly, looking back over his shoulder at her. "I suppose when the first dingo howls you'll be in my lap!"

"*Hardly!*" she said with an unresponsive little shudder.

"Don't be too sure, my lady. It's been done before tonight!"

"That I can well imagine!" Her eyes met his, shimmering strangely.

"Surely I don't read invitation in that classic face?"

"You're welcome to read what you like!" she said abruptly, bending to slip out of her sneakers, settling them neatly before sliding with admirable grace into the sleeping bag so deftly presented.

His vivid, mocking gaze slid over her studiously averted face. "Not for me to solve the enigma," he murmured with that peculiar mesmeric charm. "Besides, I'd hate to cause any more upset to the boy-friend!"

"He's *not* my boy-friend!" Perri said heatedly, coming upright in one swift glide, trying belatedly to salvage some poise.

"You had me fooled," he said dryly, "and that's the greatest test of all!" He pushed her back again and she threw up a protesting hand which he caught neatly and held turning up the palm. "Life's glorious, isn't it? So unexpected too! Shall I tell your fortune?"

"Happily you shall *not*!" She tried without success to break his grasp at once light but implacable. She closed her nails on his hand and he gave a mock grimace.

"It's all right, compose yourself! Though it grieves me deeply to break up the bold, dark image, I'm going to say good night!"

He caught the look on her face and laughed outright. "I can see it's impossible to please you. Face as pale as an ivorine. Silver-blonde. Tilted grey eyes. Bewitched with the wild bush and the night. Could it be I'm the first victim you've failed to enchant?"

Extravagantly she tossed her head so that her hair fell loose over her shoulder. "You can't be serious!" she said with exquisite care. "I'll tell you quite frankly, Mr. Faulkner, and you're obviously a man who needs telling, you set my teeth on edge. Have no qualms about that!"

"Is that all?"

"Yes, all!" She was breathing rather quickly, pale as silk.

He leaned forward and drew a slow finger across her parted mouth. "Then you've got more brains than I gave you credit for!" For a long moment he looked into her unguarded face and his expression relaxed. "Go to sleep, little one. As my guest you're as precious as a jewel to me. It's cruel to tease you in any case. A spitting kitten, if ever I've seen one, with sparkling claws. If only you could swear to the fact you won't dream of me!"

The firelight blazed on the side of his dark, rather imperious head with its strongly defined cheekbones. Perri raised herself on one elbow, too riled to be cautious. "Nightmares are no new thing with me, Mr. Faulkner!"

Next thing she was lying flat on her back and a shower of spent leaves hissed through the air.

"Whatever possessed you to say that?" he asked lightly, straightening, tutored power behind the lithe elegance, a blur of a pale shirt, live eyes.

She was driven to look back at him, mysteriously, the quality of her expression changing. Then he smiled:

"Good night, Miss Greenwood. I'll leave you on the sweet edge of agony and delight. Who can tell? You might change your mind about me!"

"I don't think so, Mr. Faulkner," she said breathlessly. "A promise I won't break! You have a fairly cavalier way with women!"

"At least I've taught you one thing worth knowing!"

Her eyes widened, sweeping his face. "Fairly damnable all round!" She spoke with far less than her usual éclat and his mouth curved sardonically.

"I'll see no one else harms you!" He stirred a little and her resolution weakened.

"I should dearly like to know why," she asked recklessly, her face expressive of conflicting emotions.

The slight rough edge was in the easy, disturbing voice. "I'll have to ask your forbearance until I feel like telling. Now, go to sleep!"

Perri felt the blood spinning into her face, and was grateful for the semi-darkness. "My pleasure!" she said shortly in a barely audible voice, and lay down again, turning on her side. But across the flames she continued to regard his tall frame with a brooding watchfulness. She would never change her mind about him. Her mind was made up. Not for her such easy, convincing mastery,

49

the dark, bantering effrontery. But where else would she ever find this particular brand of excitement? A log dropped, turning her hair more gold than silver. In a queer, murmuring, fatalistic way she shut her eyes with Gray Faulkner imprisoned behind them, the image of despotic charm. It would take the gift of strong magic to shield her from him. Romance, the game of all games! Perri thought cynically, then composed herself like a white swan for sleep. Across the wild bush the wind made eerie music to bewitch the unwary and above them in all its jewelled glory hung Jirrunjoonga, the Guiding One – the Southern Cross, the great God of the ancient aboriginal legends.

The sun climbed high out of a pure morning with all the promise of gold. It grew hot and bright, glowing from a turquoise sky. The land ran on forever, alive with the sight and sound of countless birds on the wing, shimmering in the dry heat. A flood of miraculous light. Around and beyond them the ridges rose, red-gold, towering pagan monuments edging the skyline.

Perri filled her lungs with the clean, invigorating air, aware of its clarity, yet heat was everywhere. Above, below, around them, a thousand glittery eyes mirrored in the baffling magic of the quicksilver mirage. She blinked her eyes and reopened them, but the fresh water lakes still survived, as silvery and insubstantial as a dream with a tantalising illusion of reality. Beside her at the wheel, Faulkner drove very fast – super-confident, a taut, handsome figure, his eyes narrowed against the glare, mere shocking blue slits in his dark face. The big tyres were spraying up red dust, a whirlpool of cloud castles to left and to right as they raced through the yellow spinifex grass and dry bushes, sending legions of beautifully marked lizards scuttling for cover.

Perri stared out the window at the seemingly endless horizons feeling a queer kind of exhilaration, a lift of the heart that was quite unique in her experience, as though life had taken on a whole new dimension.

"You know," she said with a hint of surprise in her voice, "I'm beginning to understand why the Outback has such a powerful appeal. Why some people never feel at home anywhere else. The incredible vastness and tranquillity. The romanticism. So much colour and brilliance. This miraculous light! I've never experienced anything like it. Everything seems to glitter, even the stones on the tracks." Her young, rather low-pitched voice was vibrant with pleasure. "The birds are fantastic, aren't they? I've often heard about it – opal tints against a diamond bright sky. It's an artist's paradise out here. I'm going to be incredibly happy!"

Gray Faulkner turned to smile at her, regarding her steadily, an indulgent expression on his dark face. "You're obviously feeling the pull of an entirely different existence. Let's hope it lasts. Some of that miraculous light, as you call it, is caught in your eyes and your skin and your hair."

Mark prodded her in the shoulder, his voice vaguely indignant. "Anyone would think you were enjoying it!"

"Did you have a bad night?" Perri smiled at him, humorously, irresistible.

"Slept like a log!"

"*I'll* say?"

"And you?" Gray Faulkner slanted a glance at her, faintly mocking.

"Utter peace!" she responded sweetly. "Silent as the desert stars. Dreamless!" She returned his glance, the coolness of her expression spoilt by the sparkling excitement in her eyes.

He gave a brief laugh but said nothing further.

"How much further, Mr. Faulkner?"

"We'll be there about eleven. Why?"

"Oh, nothing in particular. I'm content to go on forever. I really don't know what's come over me!"

Behind her slim shoulders Mark glared at her aghast as though in her declaration she had run the whole gamut of impropriety. "I'm sure the Prof will be anxious to see us!" he said tartly.

"For sure!" she pulled a little wry face at him.

"Do any shooting, Mark?" Gray Faulkner asked easily. "There's plenty of game. I take it you both ride?"

"We've hacked around quite a bit!" Perri supplied. "I want to see as much as I can while we're out here. I hope you're not going to place any restrictions on us, Mr. Faulkner."

"Why should I?" he inquired lazily, his blue eyes, unveiled, directly on hers.

"Ask a silly question, and you get . . ."

"Yes, indeed!" Mark chopped her off neatly. "Count on you to want to do the thing properly!"

"God help us, he's at it again!" Perri yawned delicately, faint irritation smothering her excitement. What a wet blanket Mark could be. Intense about everything.

"Actually, *Perri*, may I?" Gray Faulkner looked briefly into her face, ignoring Mark's flash of young-man jealousy. "I can't allow you to do just as you like. While you're on Coorain you're my responsibility, even more than your uncle's. This is the Big Sky Country – too big for little girls, even adventure-bound ones with shimmery grey eyes. Wherever you go, beyond a few miles of the House, you won't go alone. That's all I'm saying for the moment. I'll read the riot act later. I've the fatal feeling you're going to prove high-spirited."

"But in heaven's name, why?" She turned to stared at him, the lean dark cheeks, the set of his arrogant head, as if he were a proclaimed dictator.

He looked into her tilted eyes, dark upraised lashes. "The mere fact that you ask me that proves you have to be managed for your own good. Don't be misled by all this peace and silence. It would be a terrifying experience for you to become lost in the bush with only the curlews to keep you company and it can happen – anywhere off the main tracks. I'm not trying to frighten you. I'm only giving you facts!"

"I don't know you at all, do I?" The words came out at a soft involuntary rush, prompted by his swift transition from sardonic indulgence to hard male, formidable, a stranger.

"No. But you're learning!" he agreed suavely, back on course again, his eyes appraising and brilliant. "There's a mob moving over there to your left, about a thousand head. The Channel Country runs the finest cattle in the world. Not even Argentina with its sown alfalfa fields can surpass our pastures. Our secret: the Three Rivers.

The Diamantina, Cooper, Georgina, moody and ungovernable. I've seen them in all their moods – sluggish, barely flowing at all in the drought, then the entire country under water. When it recedes, wild flowers carpet the desert, perfuming the air, blowing free on the summits. Stock, lilac, wattlebush, the purple moola-moola, the pink parakeelya, Sturt's scarlet desert-pea. None of your acres of it, but as far as the eye can see, a white and gold world of everlastings!"

"You love it, don't you?" Perri looked at his hands on the wheel, their strength and beauty of shape, long fingers, lean bones.

"A man's his own master out here, as the old saying goes!"

"I can understand that," she said with charming sincerity. "No limits to the body, the mind or the spirit!"

He turned his head swiftly and pinned her gaze. "We're getting on rather well!" he drawled, answering her eyes rather than her voice. "I fear it can't last!"

"I'm generally polite to my elders!" she said blandly, changing the expression in her limpid eyes.

Faulkner gave a half laugh, a brief devastating sound. "Now that's taught me something I need to know!"

The dry aromatic air spiked with geranium flowed through the open windows, whispering peacefully. She looked back at him half apologetically and smiled.

"No need to practise the witchcraft on me, honey," he said laconically.

Mark shifted into a more comfortable position, leaning confidentially nearer his host, one hand clapped to his cheek.

"Actually, Mr. Faulkner, she's beyond redemption as far as that goes – a witch indeed, a sorceress, a lorelei. The whole scene. Ask me, ask anyone."

The colour ran up under Perri's skin, amenable to the sun, tinting a pale gold. "I'm no match for a clever one like you, Mark, double dealing out in the open."

Mark had the grace to flush, squirming a little, beginning to look anxious. "Now, now, love, only a joke. Everyone knows you're as skinny as an antelope!"

Gray Faulkner spoke idly. "You two have an endearing relationship. Can't you repair it in some way? I'd only be too pleased to help!" His dark face registered only mild inquiry, but Perri caught the wicked flare in his eyes and gasped.

"You'd do well to keep out of it, Mr. Faulkner, the danger's great!"

He received this with open mockery, a smile breaking across his shapely mouth. "I shudder to think what lies ahead!"

"Actually Perri's always acted like I'm a thorn in her side and I have to remove herself. But I won't!" Mark announced aggressively, just to keep the record straight.

"Is this true?" Gray Faulkner asked lazily, an amused set to his mouth.

"As it happens, *no!*" Perri answered soberly. "We merely shared the same seat at pre-school. His mother is my mother's best friend!"

"Nothing more civilising!" Faulkner agreed blandly, his eyes flickering towards Perri, and he gave that white disarming grin. She shook her shining pale head faintly.

"Nothing more demoralising than to have your future

settled in the cradle. In any case, I much prefer an older man!"

"Ho hum! We don't doubt it!" Mark said with his own brand of tenacity.

A little pulse began to hammer visibly in Perri's throat. She moistened her mouth and decisively changed the subject.

"Uncle Mark is very excited at what we might find on Coorain. I envy you, Mr. Faulkner, having such a wonderful national heritage on your property!"

He registered the faint word stress calmly, his vivid eyes frankly dancing. "Message received, Miss Greenwood, but even to please you I can't re-site the ancient bastions!"

"I didn't mean that, of course!"

"Of course!" he agreed dryly. "However, it's quite possible your uncle may uncover some new galleries. They've never been thoroughly investigated. As a boy I almost lived in the hill country exploring the sacred totemic sites, but for many long years now the running of Coorain has claimed my entire attention." He threw a glance into their young faces. "I imagine you know from your studies that our aboriginal artists painted for ritual or magical reasons, because they'd been commissioned to do so, or because their tribal obligations compelled them. The various tribes, of course, have their own distinctive method of aesthetic expression. This carries through to the song and the dance. Your uncle, for example, Perri, is an authority on the Pitjan-jarra with their unique fair hair. Our local aboriginals are quite different in character. Only a few of them lead the old nomadic life. Most of

56

them are employed by the station. They make fine stockmen. I suppose over the years I've seen all of the outstanding sites – Ayer's Rock, Wirindjara in the Rawlinson Ranges of the Centre, the famous Wondjina paintings in the northern Kimberleys, though I'd rate Western Arnhem Land as the greatest art centre on the continent."

"Yes, Uncle Mark told us about the galleries in the Oenpelli Liverpool River area," Perri said with interest. "They're quite inaccessible in the Wet, aren't they?"

"Just about, but well worth the long difficult trek. The caves are quite remarkable, crowded with mythical beings and creatures, the great creators, with all their ritual and magical associations, including the so-called 'Space man', and I have to admit, once the idea is suggested, that the resemblance is uncanny. They're all executed in ochres, pipeclay and charcoal. Glowing Dreamtime figures of red and yellow, stark white and black. Yet there are hundreds more sites throughout the continent just waiting to be recorded. I believe what we have on Coorain to be important. Your uncle may well uncover fresh galleries and place their exact culture period."

"I hope so – he lives for it, you know!" Perri turned up her lively, intelligent face to his own.

"And what do *you* live for, Miss Greenwood?" he asked, narrowing his eyes at her.

"As yet I don't quite know. It's enough to be young and alive!"

The Land Rover lurched into a winding, water-filled gully, overhung with filmy arches of bushwillow. Shadows darted across the silvery ribbon of water and moved into the blurred green latticework of the trees. Perri looked out of the window towards the far bank. It was adorned with a network of pure white stones arranged in an intricate series of ever-widening circles. It was no natural feature, of that she was sure.

"Some form of symbolism?" She turned her silver-gilt head, her voice filled with interest.

Faulkner slanted her a blue sideways glance. "It would take very little to turn you into a spirit woman. Yes, symbolism, by an expert. We're passing through an abode of difficult spirits. That's the work of Inkarta, our old medicine man, one of the old time sorcerers, an elder of the Eaglehawk tribe. According to my father, and he swore to it, Inkarta was one of the infamous *kurdaitcha* men."

A look of shock shadowed Perri's face. "*Kurdaitcha!* Heavens! they carried out some pretty terrible vengeance expeditions, didn't they, in the old days? He must be a great age!"

"He is! A toothless old terror and venerated for far and wide. He's harmless enough these days now his poison's been drawn!"

"He doesn't go round pointing the bone at anyone, does he?" Mark asked rather facetiously.

A look of deliberation hardened Gray Faulkner's dark face. "Don't scoff, my lad! It works all right, whether you care to believe it or not. No European fully understands these things, but anyone with experience in these matters could vouch for accredited cases. In my father's day, Jimmy Milbong, one of his best trackers, had the bone pointed at him by the Native Cat Man. One night he just rode out of camp – to die. I could show you where they found the body in less than two days. The pointing bone, in one form or another, has been fairly widely distributed all over the continent. Usually the vitim's soul is drawn into the bone, either human, kangaroo, emu, the fibula of a dead man's leg. With the *kurdaitcha*, the men used special slippers made from emu feathers stuck together with blood and a network of hair on top. What convinced my father was the fact that Inkarta had his small toes dislocated – a necessary adjunct to the correct wearing of the *kurdaitcha* shoes!"

"He sounds a thoroughly creepy old man!" Perri reacted slowly, her mind still caught up with all the old stories of ritual death.

"He is, in a way," Gray Faulkner agreed carelessly, used to such things all his life, "but I keep an eye on him. He carries out his ceremonies and sacred rites somewhere on the property. I've no real wish to undermine his authority. Besides, he's only got a short time left. One or two of the boys have fallen under his influence from time to time, but in the main, our aboriginal boys are gentle and diffident, excellent stockmen and incomparable in the bush. We have a pretty happy working relationship on Coorain and that I intend to keep. It doesn't do to suppress their ritual life, or what's left of it. Inkarta, I must admit, is a throwback to the old warrior days!"

"I can't wait to meet him," Perri said recklessly.

Faulkner smiled, the brilliant blue eyes fully concentrated upon her. "He has no time at all for women, though he just manages to keep a fair-sized harem!"

"The old devil – how decadent!" Mark burst out irrepressibly.

"*He* doesn't think so ... however! While you're here you should be able to fit in a few song and dance evenings all in their special setting. There are songs for all occasions and individual songmen. You can expect some rain-making cycles this time of the year. Songs without end, full of imagery:

'*Bilgawilgayun!* We invoke the Spirits! fresh water, running, splashing, swirling, running over slippery stones ... clear water carrying leaves and bushes before it ... breaking out, foaming, like sacred feathered armbands, swirling around. ...'

"They go on and on. In a lot of the songs, the love songs and mourning songs especially, the symbolism is very rich!"

"And the corroboree?" Perri prompted, fighting her way out of the dark web of his charm.

"As far as that goes you might be able to record some of the complicated dance steps and hand movements. That should appeal to you. The aborigines are among the finest natural dancers in the world!"

"Yes, I'd like that!" Perri said quickly, tossing the idea round in her head.

"I just knew you would!" Inexplicably his spurt of low laughter filled her with confusion. "In the aboriginal world," he continued lazily, "the *man* is fully and unquestionably the superior, with all authority and formal control vested solely in him."

"But that only tells you so much!" Perri pointed out with a faint glitter of antagonism. "Most women know

60

how to get around little problems like that. They've any amount of experience and resourcefulness. A woman in any culture is allowed the weapon of her tongue and other far more tangible assets! "

"A decided advantage in a love affair, I grant you," he conceded lightly, his eyes coolly cynical. "Personal choice is still a big factor for all of us, even societies bound by traditional custom and infant betrothals. Women all around the globe cause quite a bit of trouble! " He flashed a mock-serious glance at her. "I'm only speaking in a generalised way, of course! "

"Of course! I see no profit in militating against it! "

"Not out here! " he murmured with a gleam of pure malice.

"A man's world, Mr. Faulkner? " she asked smoothly.

"For good or bad . . . *yes*! "

"You're not married, then? " she found herself saying.

"Didn't you know? " He pinned her gaze ruthlessly, a compelling, challenging man.

"As a matter of fact, I did, and I'm not in the least surprised. I can't see a man of your type surrendering the joys of bachelorhood lightly! "

"And what is my type? Do tell me, Miss Greenwood — a young lady of your perception is bound to come up with a new angle! "

"No, please, don't trouble to turn my head," she said with great charm, the she-devil released in her. "It's always rather fascinating to meet the complete autocrat, aristocrat, local lord of creation! "

His eyes rested on her for a moment without speaking and she shifted a little uneasily. Crossing swords with

Gray Faulkner might prove utterly futile. Her long lashes fell and the heat crept under her skin. "I'm sorry, don't take any notice of me, but you make me nervous. I inevitably say too much when provoked!"

"You've still time to be taught a few lessons," he pointed out with cool detachment, his glance glittering over her young uncertain face. "Youth without armour!"

"I just knew there would be a trap!" she said a little vaguely, and shook the pale stuff of her hair. "I'll have to watch my step!"

"Nothing like practice!" he suggested, and turned his brilliant gaze to her, "though it's generally accepted that a woman has a terrible tongue in her head!"

She gave a strangled little "ouch!" flushing a little under that mocking glance, as disturbing as it was hard to analyse. He smiled, showing his beautiful white teeth, and she looked away virtuously.

"I say, something interesting over there!" Mark sat forward cheerfully, pointing a strategic finger, a quality of animation in his voice, a kind of surprised delight. "The residual from the ancient low ranges, Mr. Faulkner?"

Gray Faulkner nodded his dark head. "On your right, Perri!" There was no question she was a little in arrears with the situation and she spun her head quickly as the Land Rover left the track, ploughing across old-man saltbush heading for a tall cairn and great random-strewn boulders. Sun and shadow. There was not one without the other. It was a place of live magic, spirit-haunted; an iron-bound desiccated hill.

"Dhooraba, a primitive altar, a place of worship!"

Gray Faulkner said quietly almost on cue. "In the *eurunga*, the long-ago, the laws of life, mating and death were handed out here. It's a rare and most sacred place to the tribes and a place of great mysticism!"

"May we get out?" Perri inquired in a soft, fascinated voice.

"Why not?" he said a shade dryly, and unfurled himself with lithe grace.

In another minute they were walking along the stony slopes, where a pink-flowering shrub grew in profusion against the red sand, the white-boled, graceful limewoods high up in the narrow crevices. Diamond specks of mica seemed to glitter from every seam and crack. Perri's eyes shifted to the tall, lean figure at her side. He smiled a little into her wide, dreamy eyes.

"These places are alive with beings. To the aborigines, only the dead have homes. They inhabit every tree, every dead trunk, the sandstone hills, the secret water-holes. Almost anywhere in this sacred ceremonial land – Coorain. Come, I'll show you!" He held out his hand, longfingered, very brown and lean. In her caught, "held" state, she responded, more pliant than she knew, letting him draw her along the slope. Mark followed with his rapid, characteristic movements, swearing a little as he tripped.

Sheltered from the wind, in a deep, polished hollow, was a sacred "ring place". A rock pool, deep and secret, green as a gem, rising to the glance of the ever-hungry sun, edged by a circle of pure white, salt sand, fringed by the soft, sweet-smelling cane grass, the whole lit by the dancing, quicksilver heat haze.

Perri gave an odd little gasp. "This is where Time was

born! It has to be. Far, far beyond the limits of white civilisation!" Barely realising what she was doing, she moved her hand out to grasp Gray Faulkner's arm. "It's like a painting, isn't it? And we've stepped into it for a moment to give it balance and perspective. The frail, *human* figures!" She turned her head a little dazedly. On all sides, the grasslands spread away to the horizon. Limitless. The romance of the Outback! "It's like a foreign land!" For a moment she couldn't take her eyes from him, something in the depths of his eyes holding her own. The dry, pure air was streaming freely against them, lifting her thick, shining hair. She wouldn't have recognised the expression in her own eyes even if she could have seen it; a kind of ensnared excitement. Gray Faulkner looked rather curiously into her ardent young face.

"You've fallen under the spell of the land and much too quickly. If it's anyone's fault, I suppose it's mine!"

"Well then, you'll only have yourself to blame, won't you?" She turned on him then, a sparkling intelligence dissipating the dreamy, captivated expression.

"I should do so in any case," he agreed rather dryly, then his glance shifted to move upwards along the rock face. He moved with a stunning swiftness and edged along the great glittering boulders. He began to speak, his dark-timbred voice carrying to the top of the cairn, liquid, floating vowels – a strange tongue.

Fascinated, Perri and Mark couldn't look away from him. He threw an amused, comprehensive glance over his shoulder.

"You wanted to see Inkarta! Well, there he is – above

you, to complete the scene!"

"God!" Mark's stifled ejaculations whistled past Perri's ear. His black brows shot up and he caught at Perri's hand, holding on to it in a kind of appalled silence. "There he is, high up in the rocks. A motionless old vulture, I'll be bound!"

Perri swallowed abruptly, drawing in the grass-scented air, a tremor in her soft undertone.

"I believe he's been watching and waiting for us. I can feel it in my funnybone. The look of him is enough to make my head spin. No wonder his victims just sickened and died!"

"Extraordinary, isn't it?" Mark sounded grim, for once forgetting to chip her for her extravagance, for Inkarta, the old *kurdaitcha* man, was somehow quite terrifying, a primitive, left-over figure, for all his three spears were pointing to the ground in the accepted sign of peace.

"I'm glad we've got the big *white* chief!" Mark murmured in tones of purest relief. "Our sorcerer looks a real old vagabond and no mistake! One can easily believe the old stories of ritual death. The funny thing is, I could knock him down with one finger. He's only a shrunken old bag of bones, but I wouldn't dare try it. He'd probably sing me six feet under in double quick time. Did you ever see such terrible, unwinking eyes? I thought they weren't supposed to meet the white fella light eyes? Well, *yours* are, anyway, and Faulkner's a match for anyone. You don't suppose we're on his sacred totem ground? If so, I'll remove myself, backwards, if needs be!"

Perri got a grip on Mark's hand holding his still.

"Those cicatrices on his chest are awful, aren't they? Good gracious, Mark, you're trembling!"

"I am, darling, and I'm not ashamed of it! There's no getting away from it, the old buzzard's been practising black magic. It's been going on for thousands of years, don't forget!"

"He's got you bluffed, at any rate!" Perri said carefully, trying to return that steady milky gaze. Her eyes dropped to the old man's dreadful markings, the ribbon of human hair that encircled his forehead, the almost naked wizened but wiry frame, the dilly bag containing precious bones, suspended from his neck. The exchange between the old medicine man and the big white fella boss continued for some time, the old man's voice no more than a hoarse whisper on the wind, then Faulkner wandered back to them, careless and confident.

"Don't tell me! I can see by your faces that Inkarta gave you both the fright of your lives. Think how you'll react when you see him decorated for the more serious rituals – snake man headdress, painted and feathered, smeared with blood and coloured ochres. The lot!"

"Don't say another word!" Perri begged faintly, feeling the dazzle of sun on her head. Above them Inkarta had vanished as silently as any shadow.

Gray Faulkner laughed softly and dropped a hard, secure hand on to her shoulder.

" 'I name the blue sky
I name the Moon God, the scorpion, the sacred Mother Earth! . . .'
As long as you're with me you won't need to be frightened!" he said with sardonic good humour. "Don't let

he old power names of the sacred totems put you off. nkarta is a born actor, a thoroughgoing ham in the best radition of the theatre. He got a tremendous kick out of hat. He's been watching us for some time!"

"Did you know?" Mark asked bluntly.

The very blue gaze slid over him, unmoved. "Of course. It does no harm to let the old fellow think his presence is going undetected. In the days of his manhood t would have done. But he's very old now. He might just as well be carrying tap-sticks. The main thing for you wo to remember is this: Never show any fear or constraint in his presence. Try to appear as natural as possible!"

"All right!" Mark nodded his head vigorously. "He's only a wicked old bag of bones in any case!"

"Ah yes, the conventional label!" Faulkner drawled easily, "but he does have a certain psychic power, you must admit — something not usually associated with an old man of our race!"

"My head is spinning!" Perri smiled shakily, tilting her chin to the tall man at her side, aware of his strength and wide breadth of shoulder.

"You do look a little drugged!" he agreed. "Too impressionable, that's my diagnosis!" He seemed to be staring into the depths of her iridescent eyes. "Besides, you're probably hungry!" His hand moved lazily and pushed back the heavy silky hair from her face and over her shoulder. "Another thing, young lady, while in Coorain, wear a hat. Understand me?"

"Certainly, Mr. Faulkner. I want only to please you!"

"In that case, let's go!" he said with light, rapid humour, "I can't wait to press my brilliant advantage!"

She caught the sheen of his eyes and faltered in her step, smoky eyes lifting, her willowy body momentarily off balance. His hand closed around the soft skin of her arm, prickling it with a million impulses. He surely must feel it!

"You know," he said in his distracting, attractive voice, "I'm not sure if you're not the most temperamental creature I've ever met!"

Almost breathless with the effort, she contrived to keep up with him, with Mark jogging discontentedly by their side. What use was resistance?

CHAPTER III

COORAIN! A miniature town. The homestead, the symbol of wealth and achievement; the centre of a complex of buildings covering about ten acres of parkland, full of ornamental trees and grasses and shrubs and a lily-strewn lake; the house, a vision of symmetry and beauty, one man's legacy to five generations, Colonial Georgian, with fine slender columns supporting the deep cool veranda, paired to frame the main entrance, the rosy flush of sandstone brick, the frosting of elegant iron lace and white louvred shutters.

To Perri, it was like stepping back from the ultra-modern, the featureless contemporary to a much earlier period of great architectural distinction. Behind her Mark sat forward on the edge of the seat, apparently struck into silence in reality, avidly drinking in everything for relay to his mother, a confirmed voyeur on the social scene. Perri's grey eyes began to sparkle and she launched into sincere praise.

"The homestead is beautiful, Mr. Faulkner – an inspiration. I love it!"

He received this with a hint of mockery, his eyes travelling over her sun-tinted face, the silver slide of pale hair. "A most fortunate circumstance, Miss Greenwood! The homestead occupies much the same place in our short history as the English castle, and we have much the same feel for it!"

"It could make a man ... arrogant!" she hazarded faintly satirical.

His blue eyes were impossible to evade; a strong personality and not an easy man to live with.

"You'll have to take me as I come, little one!"

"Yes, indeed!"

He looked directly into her shimmery eyes, suavely pensive. "I can see it's going to be difficult just to keep you out of trouble. However ... the house has some outstanding features that I'll show you when I have time. No expense was spared at the time it was built and the workmanship was excellent. My father made certain alterations, modifications ... I've made a few myself without, I hope, mutilating the original design. Coorain is what you might call a well-loved house. No one and nothing could part me from it!"

There was some look on his dark face, some indefinable change in him that struck an answering chord in Perri. "A fever in the blood?" she asked, and smiled suddenly, with a charming, wholly innocent seduction.

"Something like that. At any rate, you understand!"

"Why not?" she said gently. "Most of us have a craving for a very beautiful home. Perhaps one day, I'll have one!"

"I don't doubt your tenacity!" he flickered a tormenting little grin at her. "Besides, you have a few enviable

70

graces of your own . . . *l'éternel feminin!*"

"The result of a happy coincidence! Why, do you really think a woman can get what she wants if she puts her mind to it, Mr. Faulkner?"

"Let's say I can't see anyone stopping *you* from trying!"

She shook her head a little fretfully. "This is a peculiar conversation!"

"Isn't it? But life's full of surprises. You can't count on a single day running to plan!"

The warning brought her to herself. "I never quite believed it before!"

"You do now!" There was a blue flame at the back of his eyes. He looked at her and laughed, making her succumb far too easily. Her nerve ends, her *sensibilities*, she told herself, not her brain. His blue eyes were very brilliant and confident. She drew a sharp little breath.

"I think you could if you wished be . . . cruel!"

"Now why say that?" He turned his dark head, pinning her gaze, holding it with some probing light. "I really can't allow you these snap judgements."

She seized her chance quickly, her grey eyes limpid. "Perhaps, as news will, news gets out! I've read one or two quite fabulous press reports!"

"Don't be damned silly!" The dark, devastating voice was annihilating, his lean strong fingers tightened on the wheel.

"I'm as sane as you are," she said, her eyes gleaming.

"That hasn't been my impression up to date!"

She gave a little flicker of pain. "I suppose I deserved that!"

"You *did!*" he said instantly. "But oddly enough, I'm sorry. For one thing, I don't go in for wholesale slaughter of innocents!"

"Oh!" her eyes flew to his across the short dividing space. "I would have said you had a decided lick of controlled violence!"

"I admire candour, Miss Greenwood!"

"Nothing better. . . ."

". . . in the *right* place!" he said crisply. "The thing is I detest being bettered by a woman, let alone a slip of a girl. One of my vanities, you'll see!"

"Will I?" She took a deep, even breath.

"Yes! The damage is done and no promises of immunity!"

She glanced swiftly at him, unsettled by his tone, with its infinite nuances, her sensuous delight in the very sight and sound of him.

"Beaten to your knees, and you know it!" he taunted her lazily, his eyes narrowing.

"No such thing!"

"I'm afraid so, but that's the way it goes!"

"Well, I'll endeavour to hide it ... *extremely well!*" She forced her gaze outside the window. Beauty, absolute peace. "I wouldn't embarrass you for the world!"

He smiled and swung the Land Rover into the curve of the drive, pebbles spraying out from under the heavy tyres. "All right, a challenge! I can hardly resist it!" His sapphire eyes flicked her face, then he laughed, and the excitement that laugh aroused in her remained for a long time. He let his gaze remain on her speculatively.

"This is what happens when one cuts through all the

conventional barriers, and we've certainly done that. Miss Greenwood, what *is* it about you?"

Her eyes made a long detour back from the garden stung by his tone, the light, ironic humour. She smiled with an effort, calling in her antagonism, feeling it failing against his undeniable charm.

"Have your little joke, by all means, Mr. Faulkner. I still love your home. In fact, I'm covered with admiration!"

"Well, it *has* contributed to my success with the opposite sex," he drawled, his dark head in striking silhouette against the brilliant wash of light.

"Yes, I bet!" she said slowly. "The compliments must have flowed like wine!"

Mark, in the back seat, was torn between rising temper at being so ruthlessly excluded from the fast running current of conversation and the need to preserve the social decencies.

"The outbuildings are exceptionally well related to the house, Mr. Faulkner," he said in an emphatic, knowledgeable voice. "What's that over there to the right?"

Gray Faulkner turned his dark head. "The stables complex built about the same time as the house. Through the trees ... that glimmer of white ... my overseer's bungalow. Jake Rylance, you met him. Directly behind the house and slightly removed from it is my housekeeper's cottage. Her name is Talbot, Mrs. Lorna Talbot. Her husband was my father's overseer, a fine man killed in one of those fool freak accidents on the property. Lorna had a small daughter to support, nowhere to go, so we took her in and never regretted it. She's supremely capable. I doubt very much if we could do without her!"

"And her little girl?" Perri asked in the short silence.

"Not so little. Kim's twenty-four now – Kim Talbot. You may have heard of her. She's one of our leading equestriennes, takes all the show awards from Perth to Brisbane. She's as poised and pedigreed as any of my horses, which she rides to perfection. As a matter of fact there's a terrific action shot of her on my black hunter, Narunta, in the main office – a blow-up from a press print, clearing the six-foot triple bar, eyes steady, high cheekbones, mouth very firm. A very confident girl, our Kim, guaranteed to keep her cool at the steepest jump!"

Perri had a very complete mental picture of an elegant young woman in riding breeches, tailored jacket, hunting cap, slenderly astride a gleaming black gelding. She smiled a little in self-derision.

"The wooden variety of mount is my special delight. The other kind, I'm never too sure which way to get on. It's a battle of wits to the bitter end!"

Gray Faulkner's amused blue gaze swept over her face, half laughing, half provocative. "I'm sure you shine in other spheres. Out here you'll find horsemanship is no dying art. We have plenty of polo and polocrosse matches, camp drafting, rodeos, and any number of the boys are just crazy enough to try and ride the brumbies and the wild steers. Kim's as good as the best of them cutting out cattle. She's bound to be able to give you a few pointers to improve your style. All you need is to get in a little riding every day."

"I'm here to *work*, Mr. Faulkner," Perri pointed out, trying to look suitably earnest.

74

Evidently he wasn't impressed. He arched his slanting black brows at her. "I'm aware of that, but riding is the main form of locomotion out here, Miss Greenwood. I'd strongly urge you to persevere!"

"One might have thought there were easier ways," she said lightly, provoked by his manner.

"I assure you if there were, I'd have them laid on for your convenience. The simple fact is, a horse can get you just about anywhere in this kind of country – up into the hills, the sandstone ridges!"

"I can see it's going to be an eventful trip!"

"Probably!" His voice was lazy but his eyes were very blue and alert. "In any case, it's clear you're out for trouble!"

She broke in very quickly, accepting the challenge. "I'd cut off my hair rather than do that!"

At that moment it was unbearable to look at him. The set of his head, the straight nose, the amused ironic gleam in his eyes. She let her eyes wander aimlessly through the beautiful shade trees, hearing his relaxed drawl.

"What a sacrifice! I can't match you in that. What colour is it – your hair? Ash gold?" he asked with taunting politeness.

She swung her head back to him, her eyes very clear and expressive. "I don't mind in the least hitting a man who knows how to hit back, Mr. Faulkner!"

"Prove it!"

"Don't you believe me?" she asked a little breathlessly.

"As a matter of fact I do," he said, laughing, "but I might find it too harsh on the nerves. *Memorable*, certainly!" His eyes touched her lightly, stirring the oddest reactions. This kind of conversation was unsafe, Perri thought for the first time, totally disturbed. Gray Faulkner was dangerous with an almost relentless magnetism, but then all exciting men were dangerous, she thought fatalistically. She looked back at him steadily, her grey eyes gleaming, introspective.

He intercepted her line of thought exactly, making her colour in confusion.

"Lost your tongue as well? Don't worry, Perri, I play fair!"

Never! she thought with an involuntary shiver, leaning forward studiously to study the house as they drew abreast of it, veering slightly to pull into the shade of a stately desert oak. It was very hot and the cool shade was like an embrace. She slipped a hand under the shining loop on her nape and sighed. It was all so very different! She arched her back a little, then glancing sideways caught a very blue gaze. It was like tumbling head first into space – the wild, disorientated feeling. She was no longer certain she had the degree of sophistication to match him in any way. All that lean dark vitality was suddenly ominous. Her hands fluttered in a grateful, rather helpless little gesture.

"It's terribly hot, isn't it?"

He gave a short laugh. "I have to admit it is!"

From the flash in his eyes it was obvious he was laughing at her. Then he moved with that curious lithe grace, swinging out of the Land Rover and coming around to her. On the other side Mark had to fend for himself, not a little distraught. If Gray Faulkner took it into his head to amuse himself with Perri while she was out here he could play merry hell! The competition was too tough! This Faulkner, this cattle baron, with his smooth arrogance and easy air of authority. Mark's mouth tightened a little as he saw Perri's vivid face turned up to the dominant face above her. She was laughing about something, faintly wry, apricot sun-spots high up on her cheekbones, a silver lily in her strange, bizarre background. Faulkner was looking down at her, a curious expression on his hard, handsome face, very tall and dark, broadshouldered, lean-hipped. At that moment Mark felt inclined to clutch at any old straw at all.

"I could do with a drink!" he said rather plaintively. Perri turned to look at him with what Mark thought of as a "curious kind of effort", then she laughed.

"It's all very well for you to laugh," he said crisply, "but the thing is, I'm parched!"

"Right!" Faulkner intervened easily. "What's it to be, Mark? A long, cold beer?"

"Why not?" Mark announced recklessly. Beer usually made his head ache, but he was getting better all the time.

Faulkner glanced across at him carelessly as if he had made the right decision, and curiously Mark felt a little better drawn by the older man's aura despite himself. Perri dropped back a bit, grasping Mark by the elbow.

"I'm not too happy about that, old son. So far as I can recall, you get distinctly disorganised after a few drinks, not to say amorous!"

Mark did not return the faint smile. "Kindly don't preach, dear heart. One gets older, *suaver*, every day. I can put away a few with the best of them!"

77

"The devil you can!" Perri pointed out tactlessly. "You're all right, aren't you?"

"What the devil do you mean? Of course I'm all right. *Women!*"

A flicker of relief crossed her face. "I thought something was worrying you!"

And my God, it is! Mark thought dejectedly, but said nothing. In any case, Perri was searching his face in that curious way he found disconcerting. The trouble was she insisted on seeing him as an affectionate and sometimes annoying puppy, and that wasn't what he wanted at all. Just a poison needle in the heart. No woman would look at Faulkner like that. No, sir! Not that dark face and those beautiful, white even teeth, brilliant blue eyes. The whole distribution of privilege was unfair. Suddenly Mark found himself wishing he was fantastically tall. Anything out of the ordinary would do!

Faulkner turned around to look at them, chiding them lazily:

"Come along, you two, you're among comparatively sane and civilised society!"

"That's what terrifies me!" Perri said blithely, turning up a lovely, laughing face, faintly disturbed.

"Not you!" Faulkner waited for her to catch up with him, narrowing his blue eyes.

Well then, the rest of us! Mark thought silently, and lifted his eyes to the house, seeing a woman glide with smooth, co-ordinated movements on the veranda. Almost at the same moment Faulkner turned his dark head.

"Lorna!"

"I timed that almost to the ten minutes!" the woman said in a pleasing contralto, and came down the broad, shallow steps towards them.

All through the introductions and ensuing conversation, Perri had the uneasy feeling that she was being subjected to a hard, clear assessment that contained not the slightest element of warmth or sincerity, yet there was no suspicion of a lack of either on Lorna Talbot's smooth polished features; no open speculation in the light hazel eyes. She merely smiled and looked and spoke as if she had every right to appraise every man, woman and child who set foot on Coorain. It was a curious feeling, yet it was there, vaguely chilling, and Perri tried to brush it away. The next few exchanges between Gray Faulkner and his housekeeper were lost on their visitors and Mark shifted his intent dark gaze to Perri, feeling like a mother hen with a chick, moving her on casually ahead.

"You haven't made a hit there, my pet!"

"What are you on about now?" Perri asked, well used to Mark's lightning observations, usually "bang on!" as her uncle said.

"The housekeeper, love. Mrs. Danvers, no less. Bogus as hell! That's how it was. She couldn't care less about me. It's you she's suspicious of. It's impossible to mistake her devotion to the master. He reigns supreme!"

In the shadow-free light, Perri's young face looked suddenly grave.

"You're a regular old crone, aren't you!"

"Now, now, you know me better than that. We'll finish in the hills yet! I've never met a good-looking woman yet who can tolerate another. But I've the distinct feeling that Lorna is not agitated on her own account!"

Perri drew back, staring into Mark's face, her delicate brows lifting. "Pure fiction!"

Mark nearly snarled. "Whether bred of truth or fantasy, I'd put all your faith in my sharp eyes, pet. Lorna Talbot doesn't exactly relish your presence. You're much too eye-catching, as the saying goes. You could even catch the eye of the Boss. Shining skin, shining eyes, shining hair, dazzlingly young and clean. Irresistible to some!"

"I'm fumbling around for a word to fit you!" Perri said a little uneasily. "Shall we say neurotic?"

"Absolutely right!" Mark said without hesitation. "In any case, we're being spied upon!"

Lorna Talbot's voice came floating up to them and they turned as one, seeing a shimmer of sun playing around her tall, slim figure, the night-dark hair dressed too severely for her thin, attractive face.

"You might notice the acid etchings on the door," she said pleasantly, at the same time very much the lady of the manor.

"The acid etchings on the door," Mark said maliciously in Perri's ear. "Do look at them. Actually they are quite beautiful, aren't they?" Genuine admiration broke through the sarcasm.

The fanlight over the front door and its complementary sidelights were elaborately embellished with acid etchings of fruit and flowers after a very beautiful design. Perri went closer, letting her eyes run briefly into the interior of the house, feeling the first shock of excitement. The hallway was classic, handsomely proportioned

80

with a lovely pressed ceiling of flat leaf patterns picked out in gold, running the entire length of the house and broken by twin arches leading to the main and secondary staircases.

"A mansion in the wilds!" Mark said in a very subdued tone of voice, easing his shoulders, his eyes shining.

Perri nodded. "And I hope to God your shoes are clean!" she said flippantly.

A little sound, involuntary and wordless, broke from Mark, then he grinned.

"Dreadful, all this affluence. Almost blasphemous! Look at the chandelier!"

Centre hall, a beautiful bronze and glass chandelier of Italian design was poised over a floor paved with autumn coloured Minton tiles; browns and ambers and golds and a lovely shade of blue, enhancing the gleaming polished woodwork of the staircase and the double doors leading into the main reception rooms. Yet the effect was more one of airy elegance than opulence, Perri thought, with a continuity of feeling between the beautiful entrance hall and the parklike outdoors with its many varieties of trees and shrubs; a frame and an addition to the beauty of the house and its landscape.

It wasn't a house, she concluded, that one would easily leave or forget, and it was obviously to Gray Faulkner, a consuming passion; a trust handed down from the first John Gray Faulkner who had proved himself a man of outstanding ability and a true pioneer.

"Well, Miss Greenwood?"

The devastating voice was quite near, a tall, powerful

frame by her side.

She tilted her pale head. "Very elegant. Impressive without being in the least overpowering A house with atmosphere, the true fabric and feel of a family home. There wouldn't be many who wouldn't envy you such a very beautiful estate. Tell me, is there a portrait of its first owner?"

Gray Faulkner lifted his dark head and a beam of sunlight fell over his sardonic cheekbones.

"There is! At the top of the stairs. Any number of family portraits, Miss Greenwood, all executed in a suitable and sympathetic manner."

"One of you?" she asked, widening her eyes, and he smiled suddenly.

"Not so far!"

"How inexcusable!"

He turned to look down his straight nose at her. "You're a perverse child and you could get hurt!"

"I'm nervous!" She glanced away quickly, pretending to look about critically. "I'm sure he's as handsome as you are. Your ancestor, I mean, the first John Gray Faulkner!"

The blue eyes glinted, flower-sapphire. "Do you now? I'll tell you this, little one, you're bound to find out!"

"You challenged me first," she pointed out, a little pulse hammering in her throat. "Can you deny it?"

"If it's any comfort to you," he looked down at her lazily, "I feel guilty!"

Behind the brilliant blue gaze she could almost see his mind working. Quickly she lowered her heavy, dark lashes.

"Your voice is a terrible weapon!"

"So's your face!" he said dryly. "Don't worry, Perri, I'm not so ruthless!"

She shook her head a little, her colour intensifying.

"We might differ about that!"

Lorna Talbot came nearer, Mark in her train, her eyes more yellow peregrine than green. "If you'll allow me I'll show you both to your rooms. They're in the guest wing. Your uncle is resting quite contentedly, Miss Greenwood. I'll let him know you're here. We'll have luncheon in about an hour!"

"You're very kind!" Perri said in a polite, little girl fashion.

Mark looked down, much struck by the length of his fingers. A funny miasma hung in the air. The trouble was Perri was too good-looking, too young, too volatile. Imaginative to a fault, but she *was* intelligent: to Mark, a rare thing in a woman. His eyes strayed to Lorna Talbot, noting the regal modelling of her dark head, the glistening of the thick swathe of hair. Her strange eyes were very still, but there was a certain rigidity to the quiet lines of her mouth.

There *was* something, after all, under that passivity, Mark thought, and the realisation irritated him. Perri, like some bright vision, stood in the centre of the hall, her pale gold head shimmering, her eyes like jewels, casting little darting looks about her; a child looking into a fantastic new world. It wasn't only her physical beauty that conveyed this but some quality within herself raying out; an intense awareness and sensitivity to the beauty of her surroundings. Mark looked at her with intense admiration as he had been doing since he first sat beside her at the age of four and she had taken complete charge of him. Only now his admiration was not unmixed with faint melancholy. He really cared for this hopelessly innocent girl-child. He moved quickly, acting instinctively, grasping her wrist.

"Come along, old girl, there are things to be done on the instant, and I, at least, want to see the Prof!"

Lorna Talbot gave him a smiling look that still managed to convey that there was no danger . . . *not yet!* She hadn't even called in her trump card, her daughter, let alone reinforcements. Perhaps, Mark thought with utter acceptance, his mother was right, and he really was the reincarnation of an especially old and wise Tibetan Lama. There was no getting away from the strange fact that he *knew* people's thoughts as surely as if they spoke aloud in a familiar voice. Behind Lorna Talbot's serenity and stillness there was an inflexible determinedness, a tremendous alertness. She knew he sensed this in her and it made a point of contact between them.

Perri was waiting patiently, a faint smile on her tender, exquisitely shaped mouth, and he saw the clear lucidity of her eyes, like a flash of light. Faulkner, his dark head slightly inclined, watched them all lazily, but said nothing, about him that aura of vital, leashed energy that Mark rightly judged to be fatal to women. Lorna Talbot turned her head and passed a few smiling remarks to her employer, then unhurriedly she began to lead the way up the main staircase, with spare, fluid discipline to her movements. Inspiring respect, not affection, Mark thought. There was that essential lack of softness and grace, the endearing qualities that marked women like Perri and her mother of whom Mark was very fond. Mark prided himself on dealing with facts. It would be interesting to meet Kim Talbot, the equestrienne par excellence, and country woman *extraordinaire*, though the horsy, outdoor type bored the living daylights out of him. Obviously not Faulkner, and there was the thing! Mark could even feel some compassion for the missing Kim, for he had shrewdly grasped in a twinkling the great role her mother was grooming her for. On the face of it, it would seem rather a lot to ask, but one never knew.

Perri, with her impulsive, impetuous nature, just could get hurt, but wasn't suffering as it was always said, part of living. Mark was heartened by the knowledge that they had little more than a month on Coorain, for out here life ran like a flame. This was a vast, bizarre land, brilliant with colour, heavy with strange scents. Beside him, Perri moved lightly, a slender reality, her slight breast rising and falling, a quality of gleaming excitement waving about her like a banner. A new tension! In the hallway beneath them, at ease, a tall relaxed figure, Gray Faulkner, the man in the middle, but an unknown factor!

CHAPTER IV.

THEIR third day on Coorain, they started taking impressions of the rock carvings they found in a rock formation near a permanent waterhole; a typical site for a native gallery. In the forgotten hills, it was beautiful, and so silent it was almost as if the whole world had gone into meditation. Perri and Mark, intensely preoccupied, worked without conversation, painstakingly taking brass rubbings of the carvings for transfer to polystyrene sheets. There were numerous tracks of kangaroos, emus, and birds carved into the rocks by spearhead, all symbols of good luck, and the Professor, very vigorous and semi-agile, was busy on human foot carvings, filled with enthusiasm that they might lead to a funeral site of magico-religious significance.

Overnight a shower of rain had fallen, and the effect on the desert was little short of miraculous. The sand had intensified its startling rose pink, throwing into glittery relief the bright green of its covering vegetation, the soft grey-blue of old man saltbush, the dull gold of the wonder grass, the spinifex. The sky was blue silk, shot with gold, and the wild flowers on the ridges stood up pertly, pink, yellow and scarlet, the purest chalk white, their tiny faces blossoming like children whose joy in the morning knew no bounds.

The area they were working on sprawled over an area of half a mile or so and the deep red rocks sealed in fossilized evidence of the long, long ago. The Professor broke off in his exertions to call to them:

"Over here, you two. On the double! Chop, chop! Take a look at this!"

"Ripple markings on the stone?" Mark hazarded, rubbing flakes of this and that off the knees of his jeans.

"Formed before this rock *was* rock!" the Professor agreed. "The water movements of the prehistoric sea would account for this, sifting of the sand and silt." He broke off a chunk of worn stone and held it up, pausing a little to let its significance sink in – an unconscious bit of technique.

"This is a shellfish of some kind – a tribolite, I'd say. If we set out in earnest we'd find hundreds of marine relics around here. These whitish little bits here are waterworn pebbles. Just imagine, you two, this great width and openness of desert as it used to be. High mountains of which Ayer's Rock and the Olgas are remaining pebbles, mighty rivers. A Stone Age manhood stamping the virgin earth in ritual dance. The Songman wailing over the top of the giant didgeridoo. Fascinating, isn't it?" He smiled into Perri's smoky eyes, well pleased with her audience participation. "One never gets tired of it. I know *I* don't!"

"Yet we still don't know where the aborigines came from," she said.

"No, but their physical characteristics *do* distinguish them from other human populations – not that there's one aboriginal type any more than one European type. We can only suppose the first migration took place in one of the glacial phases when a land bridge existed between Asia and Australia. No placental animals ever crossed it, at any rate. Still, we can safely assume that the aborigines are of the Neanderthal descent just like other modern races. One or two authorities still hold they are an anomaly in the modern world; a distinct line of development. Our genetic picture is still incomplete!"

"But they did bring the dingo with them?" Mark fixed his piercing dark eyes on the Professor, quick as an adder.

"Absolutely!" the Professor smiled. "Yes, indeed. I entirely agree, Durand. Our first Pleistocene visitors. Actually we have indisputable evidence from the Murundian period, as far as that goes." The Professor sat back on his haunches. "Paraloo, the wild dog, the brown man's friend and co-hunter since time immemorial. His origin lost in the mists of antiquity. The earliest white settlers left descriptions of a beautiful, pure-bred wild dog with a silky red-gold coat and a bushy white tail. It had the wolf's characteristics, of course, the howl instead of the bark. It stalked its prey silently and grated its teeth through the live flesh of its victim as the wolf does. There are any number of legends about the dingo among the Georgina-Diamantina tribes. One of their all-powerful malignant spirits, the Oore-garlee, always roamed the flats with his pack of white dingos. The White Dingo is, as you know, the harbinger of death, usually the medicine man's. In fact, the Dingo Man is one of the great totem spirits and Dingo Men guard the path from earth to the Sky Country. Myth and ritual! They form the framework through which these people see their world. By the way, Gray was saying there's a community evening coming up – *corroboree*, seeing that the word has passed into English to cover all the aboriginal ceremonies. It should be an exciting experience. I've noticed the house girls have very elegant hand movements – not that they play an important part so far as the dance goes, very unobtrusive. In the background and to the side, that sort of thing!"

"It must be a source of frustration to them!" Perri said matter-of-factly.

"Well, if it is, we don't hear about it!" Her uncle stood up, grimacing a little. "Old bones! No, Perri lass, if there are any frustrations we don't hear about them. They say nothing, never complain. Perhaps we credit them with our own feelings when in fact, for them, they don't exist. Ritual is inbred, all-important. Well, that's enough chat! Yonder to your work. You've got an hour left before you sign off. Young Kim said she'd ride out with lunch. A strikingly efficient young woman, that, like her mother!"

"Without a doubt!" Mark said waspishly, and Perri grinned:

"Get off on the wrong foot, pet?"

Mark volunteered no more, but slunk away beetle-browed, unobtrusively like a private detective, back to his work.

Kim Talbot timed her arrival almost to the second, pausing at the cave entrance, her glance sliding over the party from head to toe. Her eyes were her mother's; peregrine yellow, her face and form, similarly spare and efficient, a "closed" face, scorning decoration, but withal a slender, strongly built young woman, her dark golden tan lit with the glow of perfect good health, her long, finely chiselled mouth very straight at the corners: a whole world of difference between her as a type and Perri, who turned her pale blonde head, her young face unguarded, serene, with that curiously "lit" quality that was so much a part of her.

"Hello, Kim! How nice of you to come out to us!"

"No bother at all!" Kim's voice was very crisp, cultured, no trace of a drawl – a cosmopolitan voice. "I was coming this way in any case," she added casually, advancing into the cool dimness of the cave with its glowing walls.

Mark stood up, lanky, lean, narrow-eyed, watching the new arrival, whom he didn't like. She flicked him a quick indifferent glance.

"How goes it?" Then her yellow cat's eyes passed on to the Professor and she smiled for the first time, an action that altered the entire composition of her face. There was a note of genuine respect and liking in her voice.

"You must have inexhaustible patience, Professor. I've just about finished your book on the Pitjantjara. Quite marvellous. It deserves greater public recognition!"

"Why, thank you, my dear!" the Professor just saved himself from smiling. "To hear you say that is some compensation!"

"I'd like to think so at any rate," she said sincerely, and moved back to the rock wall, touching the long horizontal marks. "Maratjoora, the Great Rainbow Snake," she said matter-of-factly, "banished to the desert for his treachery and cunning. These are very old – birds, animals, so on. The local totems. Anything sacred here, Professor, do you suppose?"

"Perhaps, my dear. Nearly every site like this near a water-hole, especially in the desert, is connected with a myth or a section of a myth. I think in this case, religious. I'm rather hoping to find a burial ground!"

Kim shrugged her square shoulders. "You will somewhere on Coorain. In the long, long ago, Kinigar, the Native Cat Man, the mythical man of the Dreamtime, made the *kirrenderri* his haunt, killing for the sheer joy of taking life. The bush was strewn with the bodies of men, women and children; innocent members of the tribe. Then came the day when the tribal elders blocked all the springs but one, perhaps this one, and Kinigar was forced to drink where the warriors were waiting to spear him to death. The red star in the constellation of Orion is his spirit and our little native cat with the white spots on his coat from the spears is his transformed earthly spirit!"

The Professor threw up his sinewy, tanned hands. "I know that one, young lady, but you forgot Mopoke, the Owlman, and Wildar, the Eagle Man, who engineered the whole thing. The legends are fascinating, aren't they? and quite beautifully and imaginatively depicted by Ainslie Roberts. Have you seen any of his paintings?"

Kim's eyes were very golden and piercing, her mouth

firm, her chin high and resolute.

"Indeed I have! Mr. Roberts has made extensive tours of tris part of the country. The Land of Strange Gods!" Her eyes flickered towards Mark, mocking him in some kind of feline triumph. "By the way, I saw your old friend Inkarta. He's hot on your trail, stationed on one of the ridges pronouncing all sorts of secret and mysterious chants and incantations!"

"They're bound to fail," Mark said shortly, looking back at her with something approaching dislike. "He's a professional actor, even if he is travelling incognito!"

"I wouldn't know so much!" Kim said with careful distinctness. "As Gray is bound to have pointed out to you, Inkarta has the gift of strong magic!" Her eyes professional actor, even if he is travelling incognito!"

"An old fake!" Mark insisted. "In the plainest words I can find!"

Kim considered him long and thoughtfully, illogically liking the shape of his head, the close set of his ears, giving him a rather dashing look if he could only lose his mulish manner. "I thought you were more intelligent!" she said slowly.

Something in that brusque remark turned it into a challenge. Mark rounded on her quickly. "Now why should you think that? Have I done anything to influence you in any way?"

Kim's voice was dryly amused. "Actually, I think you're uneasy and you're trying to hide it!" She laughed a little cold-bloodedly. "Don't let the old devil make off with any of your clothes, even a hair of your head. It could make you very vulnerable. Important or not, belief in ritual sorcery is still pretty widespread, and Inkarta is quite a few cuts above the *nungarar* or ordinary medicine men!"

Mark bent his narrow dark head. "In that case, he should be regarded as potentially dangerous!"

"Not to us!" Kim pointed out in a honey-smooth voice.

The Professor intervened, recognising the danger signals in Mark. "Now, now, Kim, the customary thing is not to alarm the staff. What we have to remember is this: sorcery was and is used in a general way as a form of social control. You know that, Mark. A means of maintaining rules of behaviour and handing out just punishment. An infringement of tribal law is a serious offence and deaths occur because of this. Illicit elopments, adultery, breaking tribal taboos, certain bizarre acts. The sorcerer as a rule doesn't operate from sheer malice. There *is* the social control aspect!"

"Well then, the victim has the satisfaction of knowing that while he's breathing his last!" Mark said sarcastically. He started to stare off into space, feeling almost glassy-eyed with the heat.

The Professor glanced absently at him. "Deaths are nearly always followed by inquests and the whole situation is discussed in detail. Sometimes revenge is sought – a form of balance!"

"Preferably on a dark, still night!" Perri said lightly, smiling at Mark, trying to will him out of his mood. "So don't let anyone painted in ochres and covered with

93

feathers get behind you with a bundle of spears, old son!"

"Quite the most gripping advice I've ever had!" Mark said superciliously, and suddenly smiled, seeing a picture in his head.

This vaguely irritated Kim, who liked a man's moods to be constant, not a changing pattern of light and shadow.

"Actually," she said impressive, "a specific death around here is a very upsetting event. It affects everyone – the House, our staff, the whole camp. They have to change site immediately in any case. Death and its inevitability is closely associated with all aboriginal ritual. It's so much around them. The bush nurses do everything they can to teach them the elementary principles of good health, but the task is enormous, especially with the desert people. Some of them that come in have never seen Europeans. We can handle our people on Coorain. All of the big stations do. But there are so many others. Death is pretty prevalent, but what interests the aborigine most is what happens to the essential spirit – the soul. I've seen women mourners on the property go absolutely hysterical, gashing at their heads and bodies covered in blood from their wounds, however superficial, wailing in the most eerie fashion. It would lift your hair to hear them. Frightening, I tell you! Quite primitive. Part genuine grief, part simulated hysteria. Gray watches for it. They go into near frenzy. When a man dies, his wife is soon reallocated after a period of mourning, but the dead man's name is never mentioned again – *tabu*. Around the Georgina, the dead man is then wrapped in a net, laid on

94

a platform, covered with sticks and bushes and all his possessions and . . ."

"Oh, please!" Mark held one hand to his head, wincing.

"Sorry! I didn't realise you were squeamish!" Kim apologised shortly.

His eyes had a dark, hypnotic look and she jerked hers away from him. "You know *now*! In fact, to be absolutely honest, I have a very delicate stomach indeed!"

"No comment!" Perri said almost casually, knowing this to be true. She turned and smiled at her uncle. "In a crisis what say lunch out of doors?"

"Why not, but we'll have to be quick!" the Professor said lightly. "I think Mark's going to faint!"

Mark's head jerked and he spoke with stern decisiveness. "I'll take the lunch basket, Perri. I do hope you're going to join us, Miss Talbot?"

Kim's smile was tolerantly amused. "Not today. I'm riding on to join Gray."

"No matter! The time may conceivably come when you will!" Mark drawled ironically, unbelievably catching Kim off guard. She moistened her mouth which surprisingly had a slight tremor. "I'll see you all later on."

"And thank you once again, my dear. We do appreciate it!" The Professor took Kim's elbow and moved towards the cave entrance, shoulders hunched, silver head bent, a big, handsome man and very gallant.

"No trouble at all, Professor!" Kim turned to smile at him, screwing up her eyes against the brilliant light, straightening her shoulders automatically. "Goodbye, Perri . . . Mark!" She said it quickly as if to get it over with, eyeing Mark from under her lashes, but that tedious, mulish expression had settled on his dark features and she had the irresistible and quite unprecedented desire to kick him in the shins. Her eyes brightened with a certain relish. There would be time enough!

She moved on with a salute of her hand, taking the downward slope to the flat where a big bay gelding was cropping over the sweet herbage. A few minutes later they were flying over the closely packed spinifex plains with a whirlwind of loose grass leaping and dancing beneath the powerful thrust of the bay's hooves, moving into the silver mesh of mirage.

"Arrogant bitch!" Mark said pleasantly, his eyes never straying from the undeniably picturesque sight.

"Now there's a pretty thing to say!" Perri chided him gently. "I simply can't reconcile it with your normal sweet nature. Come on, let's have lunch. It looks like a feast!" She bent her pale head over the lunch basket and peered with interest into the various compartments.

"Chicken, ham, salad, fresh rolls, lashings of butter. Fruit cake. Thermos of tea. Another, I suppose, of coffee. What's this? Something interesting. No, pepper and salt. The days may come and the nights may go, but one thing is certain – we'll never starve on Coorain!"

The Professor was standing slightly above her, evidently looking for something, then he turned about.

"Over there, I think, Perri, my girl. The desert oak. It will afford the most shade. Such a beautiful, *melancholy* tree, I always think – those drooping jade plumes and jet black trunk. Take the basket, Mark, like a good lad. My days of fetching and carrying are over. It's a cup of tea

I want more than anything else!"

Mark took the basket with charming good grace and Perri followed, stooping to pick a small sandhill lily with long roots containing a large proportion of moisture. The flowering flats and the sandhills were a tapestry of glowing colour, dry and vivid, that somehow merged into a harmonious whole. Crimson flower swallows carted restlessly to and fro, chitter-chatter tirelessly, and a few hundred yards off a kangaroo hopped down the slope, its quivering nostrils uplifted, delicately testing the air, long ears twitching, a curious expression on its gentle face before it turned and thumped off.

It was deliciously cool in the shade of the casuarina and again and again Perri found herself listening to the whisper of the sands under the gentle north-west wind. The branches of the great oak rustled with a minor, plaintive note so that it seemed to Perri that she was being initiated into the subtle magic of the vast beating Dead Heart. She gazed down to her uncle, some expression on his face striking the exact same note.

"It's moments like these one feels pricelessly wealthy!" the Professor said on a long, sustained breath.

Mark lay with his arms under his head, silently in agreement, enjoying the colour and shape of the land, then he turned his head hopefully.

"Any more?"

"It takes a lot to fill *you*!" Perri commented, fluttering her eyelashes incredulously.

"A permissible eccentricity, surely?" Mark said lazily, accepting the last piece of cake. "I'm a growing boy!" He bit into it with obvious enjoyment. "Such a flood of solar energy! Wonderful light! Yet it's damn cool at night. This kind of country has a very definite character, a personality. It could become a love-hate!"

"I see you've been heeding the voices of the spirit folk," Perri said playfully.

"Hear! hear!" The Professor turned over on his elbow. "Only last night Gray was saying certain areas of the Run are haunted by the *willia-wa*, as the stock boys call them. They won't go there at night, not for love nor money, and neither, strangely enough, will the horses. What do you make of that?"

"Debil-debil stuff," Perri whispered, and got up and straightened. "I think our Kim would charge right in there!"

"Too right!" Mark looked up at her with unblinking intensity. "But what a dismal idea! She'd very likely pelt the lot of them with stones. Girls like that are real trouble!"

"She's very attractive in her way!" Perri said with utter impartiality, sounding him out.

Mark snorted and contradicted, "She doesn't stir my young and adventurous heart! I like a little mystery myself!"

The Professor scrambled up and threw an alert, active look about him. "Right-oh, sleeping prince, back to the picture gallery! You might use the frame this afternoon. I want a complete record of the domed section – easy enough with lined paper. Perri can carry on with what she's doing. I've got lots of photographs to take. There must be quite a few valuable sites on the property and I want to record the lot of them!"

Perri set about repacking the lunch basket while Mark got slowly to his feet.

"Do you know something? I'd like to stay put, but it's moods like this we have to be wary of. What is physical discomfort compared to what we might find? Do you really think that old devil Inkarta is somewhere about?"

"I should say so!" Perri answered with absolute conviction. "He's commonly regarded as being expert in the field. I might have a look around later on."

"For God's sake don't do that!" Mark exploded. "Not that you could expect to find a sorcerer lurking behind every bush. You'd think he'd confine his magic to making rain, or something equally productive. We'll have to get the Big White Boss to chat him up!"

Suddenly a bright blue butterfly with broad bands of gold and black came to rest on the point of Perri's shoulder and closed its velvet wings. Mark gazed at it in fascination. "All of a sudden, the harsh land looks very friendly. What a glorious specimen! A true Chinese blue!"

"*Nimma-gunta*, the butterfly fairy!" Perri said scarcely above a whisper, but it was enough to send the large, languorous butterfly sailing idly on. High up above them the Professor came to the mouth of the cave and looked down at them pointedly with justified resentment.

"Might we have a little discipline, eh?" he asked sardonically. "Though I grant you Coorain has a hypnotic fascination. Mark, come along, this isn't our little hobby, you know. We do have a Government grant!"

Mark reacted as though a sore point had been hit, charging indignantly up the slope, but the Professor had already withdrawn, his plea falling on successful ground.

The afternoon wore on and Perri walked to the entrance of the cave, feeling the breeze, cool as a mother's hand on her hot brow. Behind her the Professor and Mark were engaged in an all-exclusive debate. She moved slowly into the air, peering around her suspiciously, allowing herself the not unpleasurable sensation of a shiver of superstitious fear.

The sun glinted off her hair in a silver-gold sheen and rather wistfully she gazed about the slopes, her eyes seeking a figure – an old hunting warrior, a medicine man; the *kurdaitcha* man, Inkarta. Nothing living was visible. He could be hiding anywhere behind the glittering rose-red ridges, the miniature cliffs, the swimming sea of green. She moved cautiously along the rock face, picking her way over the slopes.

Phantom chains of waterholes quivered and jumped before her dazzled eyes and she straightened abruptly, rubbing her nape. What a strange land! Tension was mounting in her, fine and taut, a prickle of awareness. She turned into a narrow fissure and despairingly her heart flipped. She turned faint. She couldn't run. She couldn't breathe. She jerked her arm sideways in an involuntary spasm, her nails biting painfully into the palm.

Before her Inkarta's lashless eyelids jerked open, exposing the milky, ominous iris. He grunted hoarsely and sent the vicious point of his spear into the ground, shaggy head erect, a savage pride on his face, his dreadful presence, emaciated by the storm and stress of ages, very real. She was frozen into immobility with lightning speed, a black and primitive skill, the fabled *mulkaree* – psychic

100

terror. Her slight body shivered in the heat, pressed back against the rock, too delicately civilised for its primeval environment.

A falcon screeched harshly overhead, swooping low, its eyes cruelly bright, and it entered her head heavily to scream, but she couldn't. The heat of the sun was washing her dizzily against the rock face, the ancient eyes never leaving her face. In the Kimberleys and in Arnhem Land, she remembered wildly, sorcerers made effigies from bound grass and paperbark, clay, and wild beeswax. The image victim was then stabbed with a pointed stick and sung over until the real victim sickened and died. The falcon, the scavenger, was swimming before her eyes. What was happening to her? She could feel her eyelids fluttering in the superheated air. Was she fainting? It didn't seem possible! If she had any courage, any wits, any energy, she could pull herself away, break the senseless snare of an old man's cunning and experience, a kind of spectre-like menace. Surely it didn't require any great degree of discipline? For all his unholy hostility, Inkarta was an old, old man, yet she felt exhausted, compelled to remain against the rock in a half convulsive panic, bound by a grotesque will.

The voice, when it came, was harsh and imperative, unmistakable, down on the flat about twenty yards off. It had the instant effect of sending Inkarta's near naked figure scurrying backwards to merge into the clot of shadows that lay along the cliff face riddled with tiny caves. Stones flew and a tall, lithe figure mounted the bank with great sureness. Perri didn't look up, but gasped for breath, abandoned to relief, the sheer triumph that now she was safe. She spun her head a little dazedly from side to side, trying to break through the spell, then he was towering in front of her, brilliant turbulent eyes travelling over her with intense irritation, the tumbled pale head, the strange intensity of her face with its marked pallor.

"You bloody little fool!"

He shook her hard, lean fingers gripping her so that her head lolled a little on its slender neck, and her answering voice was wry with shock.

"I might have known *you'd* sober me up! I've been bewitched," she said in puzzled defiance. "Look at me – stupid with fright, trembling. The lot!"

His hand slid under her hair, forcing her face up. "What the devil are you talking about?" His eyes had a curious considering quality, the blue flame of anger dying to a flicker. Yet there was no trace of the devil-may-care about him, only a barely suppressed male impatience. She looked unseeingly back over her shoulder.

"Inkarta! You saw him?"

"I certainly did *not!*" His voice was flat and hard. "Only you, slumped against the rock face, obviously befuddled!"

She looked shocked. "But you *must* have! He was here!"

"If that's the way you want it!" His dark face was sardonic, and the colour mounted her skin at the sense of anti-climax.

"But he *was!* Please, Gray, believe me. He was *here!*" she repeated urgently. She shook back her tumbled hair, her grey eyes like smoke, the pupils distended.

"Gray?" His voice mocked her, its effect shattering. "It's been Mr. Faulkner up to date – and very proper. A piece of expert advice, little one. Not for the *first* time. While you're out here, wear a hat. You're obviously not used to our sun!"

Her brow knitted with delicate concentration. "I tell you he was here, just at the back of me. He heard you call out and he just seemed to vanish into the rock. If we look we may still find him. I only know he struck terror into my heart!"

There was some kind of laughter beating in his voice for all its impatience, his face a dark copper mask beneath the broad grey brim of his stetson.

"God, trust a woman to give it a little atmosphere!"

"You don't believe me?" She looked up at him with renewed agitation, non-acceptance breeding a hot passion of frustration.

His answer was emphatic without the saving grace of a moment's deliberation. "I knew the moment I laid eyes on you that you'd be a fine disturbing element!"

She seemed like a child begging for reassurance, her eyes touching on every feature of his face, and he gave a hard, brief laugh, his gaze dropping to the full curve of her mouth.

"How many days?" he asked dryly. "Three? I suppose a woman's been kissed in less!"

There was an odd disturbing look on his dark face and tiny tremors flickered down her spine. "How did *you* find out, I wonder?" she asked, and he smiled at the soft, jerky rapidity of her voice.

"A very fruitful source of experience, perhaps. But

good or bad, to let another day go by would be a wicked waste!"

A wash of something like flame closed over her in a golden tide, cancelling out every other consideration. She seemed coiled like a spring, waiting, and he bent his head and found her mouth with a sensual perfection that left her mindless under the hot sun, moving with one gesture to melting like snow into the hard half circle of his embrace.

"Everything about you is different," he said, almost derisively against her mouth, his sapphire eyes veiled. "As it happens, I don't greatly care!" His hand slid into the small of her back and he pulled her completely into his arms, his face faintly enigmatic.

The completeness and depth of her response shocked her, but there was nowhere to withdraw to. It was like drowning, going under for the third time and never caring, lost in a strange new world shot with living light. The impulse towards surrender smouldered in every vein, transmuting the heat in her skin to pure gold. She made a faint, instinctive movement towards him and he released her abruptly, his brilliant eyes glimmering between their thick dark lashes.

"Don't panic! That's it, much as I hate it, though your ability to stimulate desire fills me with unqualified respect!"

Perri collected herself with something like pain, releasing a long-pent-up breath. "In another minute I shall think of some words a lady dare not pronounce!"

"And suffer accordingly!" He looked into her face. "Don't worry, Perri, you'll control yourself brilliantly.

You wanted that as much as I did. Inconsequent enough, surely. A kiss?" His eyes ran over her very blue and glittery. "One way and another, you're a remarkable young woman!"

She threw him a glance, her eyes enormous, and he laughed:

"No, don't look at me like that! I've been tempted enough!"

"I'll look at you as often and any way I like!" she said a little wildly.

"How determined of you!" His voice relaxed slightly. "But give me a breathing space. I don't think I've kissed a nicer mouth!"

Her face was without colour except in her softly pulsing mouth. "Praise with a vengeance!" she said tersely, her voice husky, and turned her silky pale head.

"Not a word more! At least you've snapped out of it!"

"You use drastic methods!" she pointed out flatly, knowing the past vivid moments would be for ever lodged in her mind.

"We *could* try again," he said slowly, waiting with interest for her reaction, his eyes blazing into life. "What? A breathless, fraught silence?"

"Despicable!" she managed with a suggestion of cool malice, striving to get beyond the mockery of his voice.

"Fancy that!" He could see her pure profile, the shining fall of hair, the delicate tendrils at her temples. Her face was without colour except the mouth that seemed to pulse with a wild cherry glow.

"If it's any consolation to you," he said lightly, "it's all I can do to prise myself away!" The cool level tone was devastating. Blue eyes, supremely adult, faintly cynical, looked down quickly, pinning her gaze. "Now, don't hate me!"

Despite herself she coloured, a dreadful yearning coming on her from nowhere, like renewed fire. Hate you! Hate you! she thought dismally. It was too much to ask of anyone. Certainly a woman! But hadn't she asked for it? What more could she expect? Men like Gray Faulkner went through life putting women into a soft fret. It was that bright air of challenge, the glitter of humour, the sensual twist of a shapely mouth.

She tossed her head like an obstinate, irritable child, a kind of self-contempt making her speak sharply.

"I'm sure you'll excuse me now. I've had a long enough break re-educating your tastes!"

His eyes slid over her, giving fair warning. "Reckless, wouldn't you say? Your winning ways are going to land you in trouble! Did I say I wasn't completely satisfied? You ought to know by now, the price of education is never small!"

Excitement thrummed along her veins. Everything about him was so urgent, so vital.

"Rakish lover!" she said in a soft shaky voice, hardly realising she had said it at all.

"What's wrong with that?" Devilment deepened in his face, keying her to a new, strange pitch. That lazy immobility was deceptive. In a moment he would move. In the end she did the only thing she could do – the easy way out, moving off like a startled gazelle along the rock face, but without its saving grace, stumbling a little in her inexorable haste. He followed her up with that lithe vitality, self-sufficient, self-reliant, sharply amused. He overtook her easily, his mouth twisting into a grin.

"You're in a very impetuous frame of mind today! You shouldn't have said that, should you, smoky eyes? The rakish lover bit and all!"

"I know!" She was breathless, stayed by his hand, warm and hard.

"Don't tell me you dislike being made love to?"

Looking up into his face, Perri tried and tried to fight clear of the millrace of coursing emotions. Her head was going round and round like a spinning top.

"Oh, go to the devil!" she said tiredly.

"Now where else would you consign me? Answer me, Perri!" His hand closed over her delicate collar bone. "One question at a time!"

"Heaven forbid!" she said, very perverse and feminine, her tilted eyes bright as jewels and oddly defenceless.

"You're a terrible liar!" he pointed out evenly.

"I don't like you much either!"

"You mean you dislike *overlordship* – to give it an old-fashioned name. Tell me, what would you have me do? Pay court to you?" He laughed beneath his breath, his blue eyes sliding over her gilded head, something about him wildly evocative of the portrait that graced the top of the stairs. "Women never say what they mean, Perri. I found that out long ago. In that way, you're no different from the rest of them!"

Her face glowed with colour, her voice diamond bright:

"Good or bad, I'm not affording you any meaningless entertainment!"

He pulled her closer, holding her still, feeling the quick tremor that ran through her. "No? Then you'd better steer clear of me, hadn't you?" There was a highly disturbing element in his soft drawl. He tapped her cheek with a painful, stinging sweetness and left her where she stood, staring after him with a childlike concentration, with the belated vision of his vivid, mocking eyes. Obviously he found the whole situation comic, controllable, whereas she was floundering like an immature schoolgirl, ruled by her emotions. It would never do. Gray Faulkner was much, much too cool a one, with realms of experience. Inevitably he would have her baffled. She fixed her eyes on a point between his wide shoulderblades, resenting his air of tremendous natural authority. If she tried a little harder, she could work up a fairly convincing defence mechanism that should sustain her for the rest of their stay. There was nothing to be gained from deliberately courting danger except shattering pleasure ... and *pain!*

On the slope above her Faulkner turned and looked down, catching the deep indecision on her young, ardent face. There was a sensual, ironic twist to his mouth.

"You'll solve nothing, planted down there like some improbable lily. I thought you wanted to get on with your work. Come along, little one, the lesson's over for the day!"

"I hope that's a promise," she said earnestly, and he laughed and bent down to her, extending his hand. She took it, feeling the jolt right through her body, then she was standing beside him, rocking a little. The echo of her own voice seemed to float, then fall like small pebbles in the gold-shrouded air.

"A promise!" he repeated lightly, and unexpectedly touched her cheek. "And no small thing, my dear girl!"

She made no attempt to answer or to argue with him, her grey eyes resigned. She stared back at him, seeing what she thought was acid humour, the look on her own face, excited and provoked, answer enough. Yet she was no doormat for anyone. For too long, Gray Faulkner had won every contest of power, pretty girls by the score. *She* had no intention of giving in to him on any point. It scarcely seemed relevant that at his touch her whole body ignited. He was expert at that kind of thing, an innate and powerful magnetism. Acceptance would bring its own form of immunity.

She forged on with a kind of frenetic animation. "I'll go ahead," she announced briskly and quite unnecessarily.

A glitter of laughter crossed his dark, mobile face.

"Let me speed you on. It's all been *too* fascinating!"

Perri tried to ignore him, taking a deep breath, filled with an odd restless longing and consternation too. She was moving swiftly now, with curious, muffled energy like a bird fluttering at a closed cage. Something unbearable was happening to her. Tumultuous, rather desperate, it tore at her so that the peaceful, uneventful tenor of her existence seemed to be breaking up like ice floes under the golden tide that spread out over the dazzling landscape.

Gray Faulkner bent his dark head and ran his thumb

with a rare gentleness over her hand, feeling its trembling, almost as if he knew what she was thinking. The design and pattern of his life, Coorain, was laid out before him, waiting for him, bent to his will. Nothing she could do would ever interfere with this!

CHAPTER V

PERRI looked down the dinner table at Lorna Talbot, hearing the quiet, confident voice, noting the beautiful poise of her raven head, an inherent refinement and not the result of long training. A most unusual woman, Perri mused, and very uncommon as far as housekeepers went, for she presided over the long, faultlessly arranged dinner table with the slightly formal, majestic air of a society dowager of some standing.

An opportunist, Mark had very unkindly dubbed her in one of his long rambling conversations with Perri out in the sandhills, but Perri thought of her more as a strong-minded women in the maternal tradition who wanted the best things out of life for her daughter and was prepared to go to some lengths to achieve them. That didn't necessarily make her a realist, Mark had reasoned, being of the opinion that Lorna Talbot and her daughter to a lesser degree had set their sights much too high; an opinion borne out by the fact that Gray Faulkner's mother and his two admittedly social butterfly sisters treated the Talbot womenfolk to a charming, slightly patronising civility as it suited all three of them to have the domestic arrangements of the station run so efficiently, especially

111

during their long absences. The two Faulkner girls were at present touring Europe for perhaps the fourth time, no one was sure which, and Melissa Cortland, formerly Faulkner, was spending some little time with her father on his sheep property, Warrawee Downs. Kim had supplied that piece of information with a slight compression around her mouth and the muffled undertones of long-standing resentment.

Perri continued to look at Lorna Talbot thoughtfully, fascinated in spite of herself by so much calculating ambition. The glimmering peridot-coloured eyes were fixed on her daughter's face waiting for Kim to speak, to add the sparkling youthful viewpoint to the conversation, which ranged over a surprisingly wide number of subjects. The expression in those unwinking yellow eyes was immensely telling, willing Kim, her child, her life's creation, to be beautiful and vivacious, the epitome of graces, everything a man like Gray Faulkner, imperious, worldly and demanding, could want in a woman.

With a little dismal shiver Perri turned her own head, seeing a dark, handsome profile, clever, *arrogant* surely, a very white smile. The blue eyes were resting on Kim's golden face with obvious amusement, for she had a dry, faintly malicious wit. Perri's heart seemed to quiver and stop, overwhelmed by her first encounter with sexual jealousy. It was shattering in its fashion, almost as if a loved one had slammed a door in her face. How strong was her pride? she asked herself fiercely. Pride could carry you safely through most things. In a way she almost wished herself away from Coorain, back in her calm, uneventful existence.

She lowered her heavy lashes, longing to have a pencil in her hand to make a few lightning sketches of that sardonic dark head, for in this she was considerably gifted. Failing that, Perri rubbed her finger hard against the beautiful lace mat, trying to build up an effective cover of social impassivity. She wore a silver-sheened dress that left her arms and throat bare and showed the slight alluring curve of her breast, her hair sliding in a silk screen around her oval face, kissed by the sun, her grey eyes withdrawn.

The light from the beautiful chandelier was shining all over her, though she wasn't aware of it, being lost in a little world of abstractions, not yet able to will herself out of it. Mark, who normally gave her moral support, was seated on the other side of the table next to the plump, attractive wife of one of the big Southern buyers who had flown in to Coorain that same afternoon, for Coorain had a nationwide reputation within the cattle industry.

The burr of voices was faintly hypnotic, a lively blend of laughter and gossip and informative snatches. Perri tilted her head a little, trying to ease the faint sense of strain that seemed to be taking possession of her. Perhaps she had had too much wine. It was a superb Australian dry red with a character something like fresh blackcurrants soft and round on the palate and the perfect complement to the incomparable Georgina beef Coorain boasted. She wasn't used to a red, only a little hock or riesling. It had to be the wine, this floating, ethereal sensation.

She heard her uncle laugh in open enjoyment at something Gray said, heard Kim's quick retort, the chorus of laughter, and her gaze moved a little frantically around the room, touching on the beautiful carved furniture, the ivory and gold of the plaster ceiling, the bronze-green brocade drapes at the french windows. The magnificent cedar double doors leading to the drawing room were left open and she could see the shimmering magic of the Waterford chandelier, twin to the one above her head, reflected in the elaborate, gold-framed mirror above the white mantelpiece. On the east wall hung the portrait of Arabella Faulkner, the first Gray Faulkner's wife, a creamy-skinned, elegant beauty, luminously fair, who still seemed to live and breathe.

Someone at the table called her name in a gentle, amused reproach and slowly she reorientated herself, her smoky eyes startled.

"Perri darling, Gray just spoke to you, but you're obviously in orbit!" Luke Greenwood leaned across the table, smiling at his niece, secretly very proud of her blonde, shining beauty.

Perri returned the smile, faintly apologetic. Her gaze travelled, met another's, sapphire blue in colour. She had never seen such brilliance before, except once, perhaps, in the eyes of a child. A small boy. If Gray Faulkner had a son, *his* little boy would have eyes like that, blue as the desert sky.

The dark velvet voice was spiked with lazy tolerance.

"Let her be, Professor. In any case, she's much too young to remember! Though I have to admit she looks flawless with that touch of intrigue!"

Some inbuilt warning system caused Perri to intercept

the rapier exchange between two pairs of eyes, so alike in colour and shape, their marked purpose. What she saw there brought Perri to her senses, winning the battle for cool control. So far as that went she wasn't timid, frightened off by feline aggressiveness.

"I'm so sorry!" she said charmingly, her eyes sparkling, aware that everyone was looking at her. "I'll have to accept my appearance of vagueness, but actually I was lost in admiration for the furniture and furnishings. The mantelpiece in the next room is exquisite!"

The buyer beside her, a shrewd, hard-headed business man, seconded her warmly and Gray Faulkner smiled, looking past both of them to the next room.

"White Carrara marble!" he said casually. "Yes, it is a nice piece!" He looked across at Perri with open mockery and something nameless, letting his gaze touch her face and her throat.

Suddenly her dejection vanished under that jewel-bright glance. Never in her life had she known such shimmery, heart-stopping magic, such radiance of physical attraction. Until he took his eyes away she was a prisoner, a woman without armour. Love was a mirage, floating on the horizon, tantalising, untouchable. It vanished as one put out a yearning hand. It could never be captured – at least not for ever. But why *love*? She had never called it that before. Infatuation was all her heart would admit to. Not love. Not so soon nor so completely. Yet what else was this soaring emotion that lifted her with such enchanting buoyancy, this inbuilt resilience that had carried her through their few short weeks on Coorain?

She picked up her fragile, long-stemmed wineglass as

if it were a charm, holding it in front of her, twirling it a little, a winking ruby, trying to subdue her hammering heart, not knowing that she looked, in her shimmering dress, as if all the lights had been turned on especially for her, caught as they were in her eyes and her skin and her hair, the mother-of-pearl, filmy folds of her dress.

There was an odd little pool of silence and Kim's confident young voice spilled into it with something less than her usual vitality.

"We won't want to delay if we're going down to see the song-dance cycle. They'll wait for us, of course. I know you'll find it especially rewarding, Professor Greenwood. In fact I'm sure we'll witness the performance of a lifetime. They know who you are, of course, and are extremely anxious to give of their best!"

As always with Kim, the Professor found himself controlling a smile, though he had to admit it was very flattering to have a young woman look upon him as a legendary figure; a composite picture of Dr. Schweitzer, Cecil Rhodes and Andrew Carnegie. He became aware that Lorna Talbot was addressing him and his handsome, amiable face became a smooth mask of convincing deference. Try as he might he couldn't take to Kim's mother, though he saw a great deal of potential in the girl herself. During dinner, beautifully prepared and presented by the little aboriginal housegirls, he had had ample leisure time to observe the older woman, finding no reason at all to revise his initial impressions. Lorna Talbot he had come to the conclusion was rather an odd character, but a character, certainly. Her husband's death would have made the world of difference to her. Women like that needed a strong man to keep them in line. Now her ambitions were solely confined to furthering her daughter's interests, her vision of the world extending no further than the giant boundaries of Coorain.

With an effort he followed her words, prosaic enough.

"To tell the truth, Professor," she said with formal charm, "after many, many years, I've had quite enough of these little concerts, so I know you'll excuse me. I can't allow pleasure to deter me from my duties!"

Knowing the amount of household help available and how well it was organised, the Professor smiled. "A little relaxation is necessary, surely? Running the domestic side of a great station must be arduous, I know. Very testing!"

She gave a slight bow of her raven head, a cool smile touching the edge of her long mouth.

"I can confirm that, Professor, but it's my life's work!"

"Until Gray marries?" the Professor asked slyly, trying to crack that cool façade; he was an old hand at the game. With a stab of compunction he realised he had done just that, the evidence a bitter, twisted smile.

"All I *can* say, Professor," she said icily, "is that I shall serve the Faulkner family for as long as they need me – a humble but a useful duty, I hope. I came to Coorain as a young woman. To me, it's a very special place indeed. I have the greatest affection and respect for Gray. He has fulfilled all the promise his dear father saw in him. I feel I'm not unappreciated!"

Greenwood held up both hands in mock defence against the chilly tones of haughty integrity.

"Forgive me, Mrs. Talbot, if I've offended you. It wasn't my intention. I do hope you believe me!"

Loran Talbot tried in vain to appear mollified by the very insincere apology, not unaffected by the shrewd gaze that was trained on her.

"I do my best!" she said rather flatly. "Gray will confirm that, I'm sure, and of course he's devoted to Kim!"

"Is he now?" the Professor leaned forward, his voice fervent, thinking that perhaps a mother's assumption was based on nothing stronger than wishful thinking, though he had no real means of knowing. So far as he could tell Kim and Gray Faulkner, on Faulkner's side, at least, shared no more than a long and easy companionship. It was the easiest thing in the world for mothers to build whole towering castles on fantasy. Take young Perri and Mark, for example; they had been matched since their mothers were confined at the same time. In another minute Lorna Talbot had risen rather abruptly with less than her usual calm efficiency, shrugging off her daughter's pleas to join the party, promising a delicious supper at midnight, the estimated time of their return.

Luke Greenwood turned with relief to his blonde and beautiful niece who had come to stand at his side, finding an area of peace in her smoky, deeply feminine gaze, the lovely brows and lashes. He did so like soft, endearing traits in a woman!

"Oh, there you are, darling!" he said thankfully, taking her slender young arm and steering her gently through to the beautiful, spacious hallway, with the rest of the party moving slowly behind him.

"Everything all right, Uncle Luke?" Perri whispered,

still left with the stoniness of Lorna Talbot's departing expression.

The Professor bent his handsome silver head. "With the best will in the world, one can't help finding Mrs. Talbot wearing company! In fact I suspect she'll evoke a long and powerful curse upon me now my back is turned!"

Perri's face expressed her amazement. "Would you care to elaborate on that?" she asked carefully.

The Professor turned to smile at her. "Joke, darling. Of course it is, I hope. Just an immense joke. Mind you, I think she just *could* do it! Now, where's young Mark? Oh, there he is with Kim. Moody young fellow, Mark. From the look on his face, he just could be at a funeral and none too resigned to his fate. A terribly boring characteristic, that – moodiness. And no hope of a cure short of surgery!"

A flicker of amusement crossed Perri's face and she pressed her fingers into her uncle's arm confidentially.

"You know Mark's big trouble, don't you? He takes himself so ludicrously seriously, and if you ask me, it's all his mother's fault, and Mother agrees. She spoils him rotten, you know, Barbara, her precious boy child. I've even heard her call him *precious*, would you believe?"

"Yes, I have to admit mothers *are* difficult!" the Professor agreed placidly, "but anyone with even the slightest acquaintance with Mark will tell you that he's brilliant. I'd even go a step further and predict a big future for him!"

Perri swung her blonde, shining head with indolent grace. "No, really? Lots and lots of people can't stand him. All the Uni crowd!"

"Naturally!" the Professor contributed dryly. "Brilliance is never an engaging quality. It usually tends to frighten people away. But don't worry," he said with tranquil certainty. "Mark will find himself, there's that saving grace. All we have to do is bear with him for a few more years yet. At the moment he has this tiresome tendency to lapse into silly, overgrown schoolboy who wins all the prizes!" The Professor peered back over his shoulder suspiciously. "Just look at him! No, better not! Kim's an attractive young woman, yet you'd think she was offering him cold poison!"

Perri gave a small hiccough of a laugh that abruptly broke off as Mark charged right up on to them, with the rest of the house party, laughing and chattering, pleasurably excited, deciding on just who was to go in which stationwagon parked in the drive. In the end, they went five to a car, for the two-mile trip to the sacred ceremonial ground.

Somehow Perri found herself in the lead car with Gray driving and Kim possessively wedged by his side; Perri on the outside and the Professor and Mark in the back. In the purple vault of the sky, the stars were weirdly bright, great blossoming discs, and the Southern Cross trailed across the night sky like a blazing ribbon of diamonds.

Perri shivered ecstatically in her thin dress. The night was beautiful, the breeze whispering through the massed grasses, the encircling trees listening, alive with the floating notes of a night bird, sweet and clear, the perfect imitation of a bell tone.

"It's good to be alive!" she said with lingering fervour, her grey eyes shining, her hair a heavy silk curtain with a patina of silver.

"Is it?" Mark asked incredulously.

"Of course it is!" There was a sudden sparkle in the luminous grey eyes. "And night-time is the most beautiful of all – cool and deep and mysterious, like a fathomless rock pool!"

"How verbose and slightly balmy!" Mark said, bent on being obstructive. "I've never been one for inky darkness myself. Think of all the debil-debils and evil eyes about!"

"Don't dampen the child's delight!" Faulkner warned with a twist of his deeply moulded mouth. "You'd hardly call this inky darkness in any case!" His tone was easy with amused tolerance, but it was sufficient to quieten Mark.

Perri scarcely seemed to be hearing anyone, persisting with her own line of thought. "No, it's not darkness at all. It's more a pure white radiance. Koonga, the Spirit Moon, lighting up the sandhills for miles around. Such bright incandescence! It's incredibly beautiful out here on Coorain. I shall never forget it!"

There was a swift flame in the cerulean blue eyes. Faulkner flashed a glance at her dreamy abstracted profile, tilted to the stars. The soft note in her voice seemed to drift like silk through the hushed night. Some magnet drew her eyes to his face and he said with marvellous gentleness:

"You're a nice child, Perri – sensitive, imaginative. Extraordinarily innocent for so beautiful a girl. *And* in this day and age!"

"And so very *clever*!" Kim broke in with a honey-sweet murmur, her molten gold eyes narrowed like a cat treading dangerous ground. There was a faintly bitter indulgence in her tone, hinting at scheming, planning, analysing, that brought the Professor smartly to his niece's defence, responsible as he was to his sister-in-law for protecting Perri against "all evil", as Sarah had rather dramatically put it.

"As it happens," he said firmly, "Perri has this wonderful gift for living in the present. Rare, I think, and a great strength!"

"Oh, please, Uncle Luke!" Perri turned around, her smile broadening as she heard the note in her uncle's voice.

"What's bothering you?" Mark demanded, his black eyes snapping over the lovely curve of her cheek and chin, so cool and uncaring. "It's no crime, is it? You heard the Professor . . . a gift! *Another* one, golden girl!"

"Well, we'll have to ensure that she doesn't lose it!" Faulkner said lightly, his blue eyes mocking. With the power to turn my heart upside down, Perri thought, hearing the devilment in his soft drawl. "One thing we do know is, she's an incurable romantic!"

She threw him a swift, pleading look, her tilted eyes widening. "Please, please, Gray, don't talk any more about me!"

He laughed on a low, vibrant note, catching her mood. "All right, shining one, there can't be an argument on a night like this, so let us all remember our manners! Now . . ." a mock sober note entered his voice, "what we'll see tonight is an entertainment corroboree – rain-making, singing and dancing, the water totem. An entirely different thing from the sacred corroboree, from which women and children, both black and white, are rigidly excluded. The rites and traditions of the tribes are exclusively in the hands of the men. And who knows, better so! No, Perri, don't say anything! In any case, they have no poetry in the sense of spoken verse as we have, so the chants and songs take its place!"

The Professor leaned forward, his chin in his hands, his shrewd, penetrating eyes on the younger man's profile – handsome, imperious. Splendid really, he thought to himself, then he said:

"I do wish I could get hold of the old fellow Inkarta, Gray, but the cunning old so-and-so won't have anything to do with me! It's so difficult to get their confidence and as good as impossible in the time we have available. There's so much he could tell me – details of the major myths. They must be gathered before they're lost beyond all recall. Do you think you could do anything about it? I notice you're the only one he pays any attention to!"

Faulkner was silent a moment. "I'll certainly try, but Inkarta is a law unto himself and I've no real wish to change that. So far as I'm concerned he can die as he's lived . . . a tradition. In any case he's a slippery customer, isn't he, Perri? No one knows where he is half the time. At least we can pin him down to the performance tonight!"

"Um!" the Professor agreed, "and I'm grateful for that. It's extremely difficult to translate songs from one culture to another. One word can convey a whole range of meanings. The best way would have been to see the whole cycle, but it takes much too long, so we'll have to content ourselves with a section of the myth!"

"I think you've accomplished a great deal, Professor," Gray Faulkner said comfortably. "You've covered a considerable amount of ground with the rock carvings and their interpretations!"

"And for that we can't thank you enough!" the Professor returned warmly. "Your help and co-operation, throwing open the library to us has been invaluable, Gray! And this young woman with her encouragement!" the Professor leaned forward to pat Kim's yielding shoulder, and received a slanting smile.

"Think nothing of it, Professor!" Faulkner said with smooth sincerity. "Besides, we can't afford to withhold details of our national heritage, now can we, Perri?"

A little colour rose to her smooth, silky skin. "You've never forgotten it, have you?"

"No!" he countered dryly.

"What's that?" Kim demanded, looking rather piercingly from one to the other.

"Classified stuff!" Faulkner laughed softly and pointed out the window. "The lights from the firesticks coming up now. That wall of dense green marks the creek. It's the haunt of the fairy folk and well sheltered from the wind. The housegirls call it the Lily Place and when we get there you'll know why. It's usually covered with great ivory waterlilies. Mostly they just sit like clouds on the shiny green surface. The trees lining the banks are acacias, tea trees and the bauhinias. *Their* trunks are studded with little round notches holding that everlasting favourite, the witchety grub. The great moth lays the eggs on the bark and they burrow in. They're about four inches long in the Lily Place, fat and juicy, with a sweet almond flavour."

"Ugh!" Perri gave a graceful little shudder. "Have *you* ever eaten any?"

"Certainly!" the shapely mouth grinned. "When I was a boy. Dozens of them. I'd try anything – insatiably curious!"

"And you, Kim?" Perri looked at the rather rigid profile of the girl beside her.

"Of course, why not?" Kim parried with something approaching amused contempt. "They're just as much a delicacy as frogs' legs and snails!"

"And I'm sorry to relate I couldn't manage *them*, either," Perri retorted in a limpid voice. "Not if you heaped praise and money upon me!"

"I must tell you about the time we feasted on fresh young crocodile's tail," Faulkner said blandly.

Perri shot a quick look at his dark face, the gleaming eyes. "I see the way it is!" she said lightly, "and you win! I dissociate myself from the conversation!"

"Chicken!" he said, and grinned. "Expect to hear it again!"

"You're no bushwoman, are you?" Kim began, but Faulkner held up a silencing hand.

"Listen!"

Thrown up on the night wind came the sound of the tap sticks and the spirit drums, growing in volume as they approached the ritual ground. A wallaby jumped out of sight as the two vehicles slid into the pit of darkness under the spreading eucalypts. Doors opened and shut, there were muffled, laughing consultations, Gray got everyone organised, then they all stepped out on to the springy cane grass moving towards the open savannah, silvery in the moonlight.

"I hope we don't meet up with a raiding party!" Perri heard Mark mumble under his breath, but she missed her uncle's reply, graphic enough to silence Mark. She moved ahead silently like a shadow, spirit-like, ethereal in her floating, filmy dress, feeling a wonderful sense of excitement and anticipation, a shiver of primitive awareness.

"Steady!" she felt her arm lightly but implacably held, a dark velvet voice near her head. "Whether you like it or not, you're stuck with *me* for the night."

She spun to face him and looked up into his dark face. It was like a free-fall through space. She gave a little panicky laugh, almost melting to his touch.

"Then I'm lost!" she said breathlessly.

"True enough, and I planned it!" he murmured with soft arrogance. "I want you right where I can see you, somewhere near my shoulder!"

"But, Gray . . ."

"Come along, doe eyes!" His tingling grip tightened with its disturbing intimacy. Somehow they had bypassed the long road of a lengthy acquaintance only to arrive at the same point. He was deeply familiar yet utterly strange! She might have known him in another lifetime or a split second in space. Obeying some instinct for survival, she struggled a little.

"I always get my way, Perri," he said with gentle emphasis. "Ask anyone!"

"I know it! But don't make *me* your scapegoat!"

His eyes swept her face. "You're crazy and you know it! Besides, it was you that put that lovely slender neck into the cage. Come on. Come quietly. Just the two of us!"

She resisted a minute longer, tilting her head to him, her eyes sparkling like ice crystals. "You might have some explaining to do. Have you considered it?"

"Now what's *that* supposed to mean?"

"Oh, never mind!" She evaded that brilliant glance, shaking her head rather fretfully like a frustrated child. "You're beyond redemption in any case!"

He drew her about swiftly, with a wonderful economy of movement, walking steadily just ahead of the group. "Now dammit, you can't possibly know that! In my position a man always gets talked about. When I *don't* is the time to worry!"

"Yes, indeed! I'm aware of that. I've heard a whole chorus of. . . ."

She shivered uncontrollably as his hand slipped under her hair, closing over the nape rather painfully.

"You're not clear of Coorain yet, honey. So watch yourself! Fight out in the open. No double talk!"

She relented with grace, tilting her head back against his hand. "Better still, I won't fight at all! I admire you much too much, Mr. Faulkner!"

"That's my girl!" he said gallantly, his eyes gleaming over her face. "I can't pretend I'm not overjoyed to hear it. I must be more persuasive than I know!"

"Oh, you're *that*!" she said in a voice so low he had to bend to hear it, then he laughed.

"Come on, little one, let's go! While you're with me,

you're trapped!"

He took her hand firmly, regardless of at least one frozen segment of his audience, and led her down the sloping bank. The firesticks were burning brightly as they came down on the winding, tree-lined watercourse, thrusting with pale, waxy lilies, all but closed for the night. The air was heavy with the scent of native boronia, the wild limes, the crackling, burning timber of the holy fire. The giant didgeridoo boomed three queerly pulsating notes in greeting to *byamee*, Faulkner and his guests and the sand drums set up a rattling tattoo, magic over the white man's name. Perri looked dazzled at the blazing, dancing flame, starting a little as lines of decorated dancers emerged from the shadows, a solid phalanx of brown bodies, gleaming with goanna oil, encircled with ochres, white and yellow and crimson; the Song Men stood directly opposite, ready to begin their chanting, eager to enact their timeless Dreamtime drama under the stars and the harkening bush.

Faulkner moved down towards the dry packed sand with Perri, turning to ensure that his guests were doing the same, then he stood perfectly still, holding up his hand. A twirling bull roarer gave a mighty shriek and from the latticework of acacias stepped a fantastic, hunched figure, shuffling slowly into the circle of firelight, an elaborate headdress of black cockatoo feathers tipped with flame and imperial yellow and red rising like a whirlwind around his grotesque head, feather-wrapped wrists and spindly ankles, emaciated torso decorated with fluffy birds down a sacred and powerful *mullee* stone swinging from his neck. Inkarta, the old *kurdaitcha* man!

For an instant, Perri felt like running, closing her eyes and blindly running to some quiet dark corner, then a hand moved to her shoulder like a talisman and she straightened and gazed down at the old medicine man. A group of dancers stamped forth with great vigour, throwing up a glitter of dust and dry leaves, bowing before their tribal leader with great respect and a suspicion of primitive fear.

Perri found herself shivering in fascination and the lean, strong hand on her shoulder tightened, an assurance that everything was all right and authority would never go out of *his* hands. Her dazzled eyes moved to the outskirts of the holy fire where the women and children were grouped, but even the excited jabber of the piccaninnies had fallen into a deathly quiet.

Inkarta was watching them closely, his eyes mere slits beneath the pronounced brow ridges, then with painstaking ceremony he saluted the white man, Faulkner, all-powerful usurper of sacred ground, ignoring the other white ones staring in open fascination, the ancient, deep-set eyes unwinking. He waited for his greeting to be returned with the same elaborate ceremony, then with pride and decision still flashing in reflected crimson from his fiery old eyes he allowed himself to be led to the tribal place of honour far removed from the lowly women and children.

Once seated he waited for Faulkner to give the brief command to his own people, who sank without so much as a whisper on to the thick *namma namma* grass, then he clapped his knotted hands dryly together and the performance began. Songs from the Dreamtime! The

Dreaming, an integral part of aboriginal philosophy; the time when the Earth was plunged into eternal darkness and the great Dreamtime heroes came forth to give shape and colour to the world.

The myriad lighted firesticks danced and gleamed in ghostly fashion, illuminating the flickering, trembling scene. The dancing was flawless, the wailing chants eerie, soft and sibilant, almost falsetto, and over all, the spine-tingling voice of the drone pipe. Some of the married women of the tribe had clapping sticks which they rattled together in time to the music, while others pounded the ground rhythmically with a length of bound paper-bark, or beat the possum skin drums with the flat of their long-fingered, elegant hands.

On the other side of the holy fire, the old men of the tribe sat in a spirit circle ringed around with little white quartz stones, beating boomerangs together with disciplined precision. It was a strange vast land; the Lily Place, a flowery temple! Perri slipped a hand over her clamouring heart, unaware of the light, brilliant glance that slipped over her from time to time, checking her reactions. The imagery of the rain magic singing was not difficult for her to follow, the brown man's way of expressing himself in relation to one of the harshest environments on earth.

Image after image was projected by the dancers and Songmen combining as one ... clouds banked and massed, the wind blew from a favourable quarter, then came the quick patter of rain. Streams and billabongs started to run, faster and faster, bubbling and flowing, soaking the earth. *Storms!* Tongues of lightning, flickering and twisting, flashing in and out of the trees, the roaring voice of the God of Thunder. . . .

The symbolism was striking, the interpretation impeccable, achieving an enormous impact with the wild bush as a setting a star-studded backdrop, the whole scene pervaded by the heady, perfumed aroma of the grasslands. It was all so vastly different from a conventional European ballet but no less stylized, no less dynamic, no less profound. The chocolate-coloured faces of the young lubras and their babies gleamed in the firelight, hypnotically entranced. They were all singing now, even the piccaninnies had set up their own little cacophony. One dusky-skinned belle, a circlet of plaited reeds drawn tightly about her brow, a challenging twist to her taut, shapely body, leapt to her feet with a spirited swing of her hips, huge black eyes glistening, black curls a-riot, only to fall to the ground again, fearfully subsiding, as Inkarta turned his curiously dead eyes upon her, the brilliant tips of his feathered headdress waving.

Perri shivered convulsively in empathy with the crushed spirit of the little would-be dancer. She looked quickly along the intent ivory faces of her own people. They all looked spellbound, even Mark who surprisingly had lent Kim the support of his shoulder. The wife of one of the buyers, the plump attractive brunette who had been so voluble at dinner, was clutching the lustrous strand of pearls at her throat with no apparent thought for the frail strength of its diamond clasp, her greenish-blue gaze glittery with excitement, savouring this primitive spectacle on such a famous property as Coorain; a story to dine out on for months.

The hours flew past with no break, no faltering on the part of the dancers, the rhythmic intermeshing of the instrumentalists. Perri glanced sideways into Gray Faulkner's forceful dark face, seeing its strength and vigour, qualities far more striking than easy good looks. Something inside of her seemed to unfurl like a sleeping white bird spreading its wingtips. It was a moment of passionate dedication when she came to terms with herself, the demands of her own vivid nature. At that moment he seemed more precious than life itself to her. She drew in her breath sharply as if in actual physical pain and he turned his dark head, catching and holding the strange intensity of her expression. A quick lick of triumph lightened his eyes so that they were dazzling, searing her. . . .

"Incredible, isn't it?" he asked on a deep, vibrant note, and she knew he didn't mean the performance.

She nodded, unable to speak, bemused by the assault on her emotions. Her eyes moved without volition to the curve of his mouth. Everything about him was so deeply disturbing, impossible to do without, like a dangerous narcotic. Addictive! The firesticks cast triangles of light over his face emphasising the hollows under the dominant cheekbones, the lines from nostril to mouth. It was a face no woman could swerve from its purpose. All her intuition grasped at that fact. His glance held hers, so level and direct she couldn't break away. Then he gave a low laugh and turned his dark head as if her unguarded face had given him all the answer he expected.

A jumbled, baffled hope-dread rose in her. She was making it all so easy for him, and what did she really know of him? Because she had experienced a lightning revelation, it would be little short of insanity to imagine it had been the same for him. Women were the emotional ones, the romantics, living on their hopes and their yearnings. Not men. Not a man like Gray Faulkner who had more important things to think about. She slanted a glance at his arrogant profile, feeling drugged and suspended in time.

Leaf shadows fell across his face, copper-bronze. It was easy and mocking with that wicked flash of devilry. She couldn't accept it, but she had to. He was only waiting for her to fall into his lap. The old cat and mouse game he had mastered to perfection. It was just as Mark had tried his best to warn her against. Gray Faulkner could only hurt a woman, with only half his mind given over to the operation.

She jerked her head back to the performance, trying to salvage a little pride. The deep, primitive notes of the drone pipe seemed to pulse like a heartbeat on the wild night. The dancers and singers were fatigueless and she felt herself becoming overwrought, in a mild kind of anxiety state induced by the throbbing persistence of the sand-drums and the clatter and clash of the boomerangs. She moistened her lips with the tip of her tongue, a pulse beating in her white throat.

Just as she thought she could bear it no longer, it was over! Even the mouths of the dimpled, chocolate-skinned cherubs were closed. The bush became breathless. The dancers stood like stones, until Inkarta, a petrified old figure, allowed himself to be helped to his feet, signifying with one imperious gesture that the performance was over. Within minutes the wall of men, women and children had fallen away, moving stealthily into the star-studded, purple anonymity of night. The clearing was open and deserted; flower-scented, the silence vibrating with remembered sound.

"We'll go back now!" Faulkner said without hesitation. "No need to ask if you've all enjoyed yourselves!" His glance swept around, his white smile flashing. Everyone was moving now, rather slowly, as if still in a trance, stretching a little, not bothering to make conversation. That would come later when the spell had worn off.

Faulkner checked his watch with finality and the stragglers collected themselves, moving up the bank. He looked down and extended his hand to Perri, who still clung to the grassy bank like some night-blossoming wild flower.

"I've seen this sort of thing many, many times before. It's obvious you haven't! The after-effects are all over you. Tantalising really, but you'll have a night of odd, fragmentary dreams. Come along, little one, or we'll see in the Dawn Star!"

Something in his voice, some sensual element, made her say a little wildly:

"Why not?"

The touch of his hand was a quivering dart of fire and she trembled, turning up her face to him.

"You don't mean that, grey eyes!" he countered, his eyes narrowing. "It's common knowledge that women are erratic in the extreme!"

"Some of them, not me!" she said passionately.

He steadied her with one hand on her shoulder and she stared up at him, her breath shuddering to quietness at

134

that fatal touch, her spine prickling, every nerve in her body overstrung with the oddest forebodings.

"Do you do this on purpose?" she asked, almost childishly fearful of the answer.

"What?" His brilliant gaze was full on her, dominating her, conveying that about *him*, she knew absolutely nothing.

"Poor baby!" he said in a dark, detached voice.

It stifled her. She swayed towards him, an urgency in her, her eyes glittery with tears as if she had been deliberately and rather cruelly led astray.

"Poor *baby*?" she echoed, gritting her small white teeth. "I'm only sorry my reactions disappoint you, if that's the kind of stimulant you need!"

"Witch!" he said mockingly, "for want of a better word!" He held her lightly, ignoring her agitated little:

"I love being flattered!" She jerked away from him and he tautened instantly on the verge of some kind of explosive action, then he relaxed, head up, eyes narrowing, drawing her up the bank in the wake of the others who were looking back rather curiously.

"You're going to pay for that, Perri!" he said in a soft, informative undertone. "I promise you that!"

The vibrant, so patently false amiability of his voice was dangerous and she shook her head in rippling disbelief, unwilling to concede him another victory.

"I don't *think* so, Mr. Faulkner!" she said with hardy price, rebellion a hard knot inside her, but even her words had a false, phantom ring.

His glance pinned her, brilliant, intimate, terrifyingly self-assured. "Don't waste your breath!"

She felt herself go white with the shock of it, bringing her to a slamming halt, back against her shoulder, her hair spinning out to haze his cheek.

"Played right into my hands, haven't you?" he drawled, his eyes like diamond chips.

Anger died in her. She was frightened now, fighting to regain his teasing indulgence. "Oh, please, Gray!"

"No bribery!" he said tersely, his eyes on her face. "For once all your wild premonitions are right!"

His tone was hard and goading, but tremors of a strange perverse excitement ran through her.

"Everyone's ahead of us, haven't you noticed?" he pointed out, the steel glinting through the black velvet. "Mark, for instance, has stumbled at least twice. Come along, Perri, I'm not quite mad enough to do as I want. *That* can wait. I've all the time in the world and you're going no place!"

"Do you ever say what you really mean?" she implored him, almost running to keep up with him.

"One day you'll have no cause for complaint! Now be a good girl. I'm achieving an unbelievable degree of self-control myself, but you couldn't be expected to know that, you feather-witted child!"

It could have been a thrust or a warning, but the sharp attractive note of humour in his voice defeated her. She nodded, her body relaxing, allowing herself to be compelled across the springy grass as if she were no more than a troublesome child – feather-witted, as he had called her. She could only second his scathing analysis. Somewhere, somehow, she had made a disastrous error. Her only hope now was to retreat. What else was left?

CHAPTER VI

AFTER breakfast next morning, Mark walked out on to the veranda, leaning over the wrought iron railing looking out over the perimeter of the garden. There was an odd quality to the light that morning. Everything was crystal clear, accurate, clear as a bell, without the usual heat haze. A slight breeze blew in from the east, fanning the beautiful ornamental grasses, ruffling the crimson flower tops, the names of which only jogged at his memory.

He strolled down the stairs apparently unconcernedly, walking towards the flower beds, whistling tunelessly through his teeth though he knew he was under observation; like a man to the gallows, he thought wryly. Lorna Talbot, he had long since discovered, kept them all under surveillance, especially Perri. That hopelessly innocent girl-child just went her way always framed in the older woman's gun sights – an observation Mark found unwise to ignore. There was something between Perri and Faulkner. A glitter of physical radiance, perhaps no more, but together they attracted and held the eye, each in their own way with a kind of perfection, a stunning physical elegance and vivid, vibrant personalities. It was an unpalatable fact, but not only opposites attracted.

He caught a flicker of movement from the corner of his eye and turned his head. Kim Talbot! Now there was a decidedly odd girl. A mixture of quick jealousies and resentments and a tentative friendliness like a very young actress pushed into the wrong part. She caught sight of him and waved her hand, her smooth, tanned face bright with health, slim and very attractive in a checked cotton shirt and narrow jeans.

"What the heck are you doing? Picking flowers?"

That jolted him. He looked at her indignantly, his good-looking face beginning to scowl. "To hell with that! I'm just thinking my own thoughts!"

"Now, now," she said soothingly, "don't get heated, though it makes a nice change from your usual inertness!"

He almost gasped blinking his thick, very long eyelashes. "What a very forthright young woman! You can't have many friends!"

"Enough, sonny, enough!" she said comfortably. "You in your own small way are not unworthy of my attention!"

" 'Struth!" he said involuntarily, "you're interested, then?"

"I am!" she retorted blandly, liking the set and shape of his head. "In fact, if you smiled like that more often we could be friends!"

Mark continued to smile, transferring his weight from one foot to the other, young-man style. "Oh, let's be friends, by all means. The selected élite!"

For no apparent reason this appeared to upset her. "You find the idea repulsive?" she asked quickly, dipping her head.

"For God's sake, girl!" he said shortly, something in her voice getting to him, "not at all! *Inspiring!* Given time, I'm sure you'll turn out trumps!"

"Now, that's the right response!" She looked up at him, her golden eyes gleaming, with only a little irony. "What about coming out on the shoot with me?"

Mark nearly, but not quite recoiled, never one for actual bloodshed. "You're joking!"

"Of course not!" she said quickly, completely matter-of-fact. "I often do it. I'm quite capable, believe me. We'll take two of the stock boys along. I realise it's not quite your scene!"

"Oh, lady, you're so right!" he murmured dryly, still curiously loath to back out. Her eyes had never moved from his face, sizing him up, and he said stubbornly:

"Come on, out with it! What's on your little mind? Let's have it on the chin. I'm prepared to listen to anyone who can tell me something I don't know about myself!"

Inexplicably she began to laugh, a charming carefree sound. "Not now, Mark, my mind's not really on it. Please come. I promise you'll come to no harm. Not with me!"

"Heavens, I thought that was what you were testing for. I'd hate to play poker with you, Talbot, you have such a nice straight face!"

"What a recommendation!" she said with a twisted little smile. "I knew you'd written me off as completely

139

unfeminine. It's very hard to compete with someone like Perri around!"

He looked at her in astonishment, cupping her head, staring at her full face. "Are you crazy? You're a very attractive girl! Why, when I see you going over those jumps on that black hunter, I can't take my eyes off you!"

"Oh, I'm good at some things!" she said wryly. "Come on, disillusion me, tell me you're not coming!"

"Try me!" he said masterfully. He grinned at her suddenly and she held out her hand and he caught at the fingertips. "Just don't use me for target practice! You realise the foul temper I have!"

"But just consider mine might be better!" she said instantly, in her characteristic faintly arrogant fashion. There was an odd little silence and she looked back at him a little warily. "Do you dislike my speaking so frankly?"

"I've never objected to good clean fun!" he said lightly. "Besides, could I stop you?"

"Probably not!" She bent her glossy dark head, kicking at a tuft of grass. "I've always been like that. In fact that's exactly the sort of person I am – blunt in everything!"

"Well, well, fancy *you* knocking yourself," Mark said with open admiration. "Why, bless your innocent little soul, in lots of ways you've tremendous finesse. Now, do we get started or not?"

She brightened visibly. "As soon as you're ready!"

"Good!" he said carelessly, "but just have a care!"

"That's a deal!" She had resumed her usual business-like expression, but he refrained from smiling. "I'll chat up the boys," she added with considerable panache, "and meet you at the stables!"

"You know," he said flippantly, without any fixed idea in mind, "you're exactly the sort of girl I need!"

A wave of heat hit her. It mantled her face and throat, turning her into a softer, so vulnerable version of herself, one she scarcely knew existed and obviously not Mark, judging from his expression. Then she turned about swiftly, wasting no time, and after a startled minute Mark too made a run for it, and disappeared inside the house. The Prof could spare him for a few hours. They were well ahead. Besides, he had the idea that he might enjoy himself, allowing for a few grisly moments. There were mysteries of life he had yet to plumb and a variety of characters to suit them. Kim Talbot, in her fashion, was not unworthy of *his* attention!

By mid-morning, the whole landscape had sprung into vivid life witth an elaborate and varied tapestry; overtones of an ancient heritage, its magic and sometimes cruel rites. In the near distance, the mirage was about, leaping like a flame, floating optical illusions that fast disappeared as one rode into them. Even the air seemed to vibrate, drumming sheer excitement into the bloodstream, so that the horses too shared the same sense of intoxication, prancing and reefing, scattering the gold and white daisies that swam over the tops of the grasses.

Whatever life lacked in the Outback, it wasn't *meaning*, Perri thought blissfully, bubbling over with a dreamlike happiness and joy in the morning. She headed her dainty little mare towards the shade of a flowering grove of bauhinias, her eyes following a curious movement; a pair of tawny gold dingoes on the run from the scent of man and horses, invaders into their wild life. From the bend of some hidden gully came the call of the velvety wedgebill, a true *bel canto*, limpid on the air, call and answer, sealing her off in her strange new world.

The little mare twitched her silver tail with a sweet-tempered snorting, and Perri slipped from the saddle, caressing the satiny neck, unconscious of the dreamy sweetness of her own expression. Her wide-brimmed cream gaucho hat slipped down on her back, hanging from its strap, and she felt the slight tug of the breeze through her hair. The stock-scented air was cool and balmy; leaf patterns flickering behind her momentarily shut eyelids. She opened her grey eyes again to the polished light, the tops of the trees glittering in the filtered sunlight. Overhead birds fluttered downwind, then soared to the rising draught of air, beautiful birds, the wonderfully tinted *nahleens*, the Princess Alexandra parrots with their glowing opal colours. Some kind of devil's music seemed to float out from the sandhills, perhaps from some secret watering place; they were coming out of the *marawalla*, the soft country of green herbage and grasses and skirting the less hospitable parts of the Run.

Right over on the western horizon by the graceful, curving chain of waterholes, slender spirals of dust rose and circled, then vanished slowly as a mob was moved on to fresh grass, the voices of the stockmen carrying far and wide in the rarefied air, as if they were much closer at hand. Perri found herself overcome by a blissful lassitude, the effect of the golden-green shade after the shining glare of the sun. She sank on to the blossom-strewn grass, her shoulders curving forward, her hands locked over her knees.

Some little distance off, her uncle and Jake Rylance were having a muttered confab about the faint tracks that braided the red sand, and behind them, with one aboriginal stockboy, Gray Faulkner sat his beautiful black stallion with the relaxed insolence of the expert, his stetson with its richly ornamented snakeskin band tilted to a rakish angle. He looked quite extraordinarily handsome, his skin polished bronze, his thin open shirt almost the same vivid blue as his eyes. The now familiar exhilaration swept over her, the desire to just sit and stare. She would never get tired of the sight and sound of him, even allowing for that little tangible air of arrogance, the high-bred, temperamental set of his head, the turbulent dark vitality that was so much a part of him. He was Gray Faulkner. He owned every inch of this vast, prosperous station. She could hardly expect him to be as other men.

Almost at the same moment, he lifted his head alerted by something she could only guess at. Then he rode towards her, cutting through the heat haze that moved in ribbonlike bands across the line of her vision.

"Get up, Perri. That's no place to sit!"

"But why? It's beautiful!" She leaned back on her palms, staring up at him with a mixture of sparkling provocation and defiance. What was it about him that made her want to argue? Nothing she clearly understood.

"There are better places to air your opinions!" he said briskly, a twist to his mouth, blue eyes full of mockery.

She hesitated for a fraction of a second, her face faintly mutinous, and he dismounted with effortless energy, his dark face taut and watchful.

"Of course! You *must* have the last word, even if it's silent! A powerful, irrepressible impulse in a woman. Up, Sleeping Princess!" He bent over her with a trace of violence and she seemed to wilt a little like a flower on a stalk, very much aware of his height and strength.

Laughter was suddenly in his narrowed eyes. He passed a hand in front of them and smiled:

"I wouldn't have missed that for the world! That little nervous shudder. On occasions, you're a meek enough child. Now, are you going to wake up?" He put out his hand and swung her to her feet with no pretence at gallantry, his touch like a trail of fire. The oddest little tremors flickered down her bare arms.

"Silenced by the master's hand! Do you mete out this treatment to everyone, Mr. Faulkner? What have *I* done to incur your displeasure? Questioned the voice of authority?"

He shook his head gently. "Don't be fooled into thinking you can sting me with sarcasm. The rules might be rigid, but they're fair! Consider that in a few distracting weeks you've broken more than your share of them!"

"*Have* I?" Her voice was feline, spiced with faint malice. "It's a case of toe the line or else! I wonder why you think that so important?"

He didn't move, but she felt the change in him, a kind of lithe tension. She broke off, blinking a little uneasily, disconcerted by his steady, glittery gaze. It was a brief moment, but to her it seemed endless. "Why look at me like that?" she said, her voice wavering. "You don't practise hypnosis, do you? Or if you intend to beat me, kindly explain yourself first!"

He gave her a complicated sort of smile, only part mocking, moving one hand in one of his dominating gestures. "As it happens, I don't have to do either. You're much too fascinating, with a way all your own. I've always had this irrational liking for ash-blondes!"

His eyes were a brilliant shock of colour, filled with vivid, blazing lights and an unmistakable careless arrogance as though she were no more than a tame bird, well in hand. It was all just a game, to be ended as suddenly as it had begun. She looked back at him in slight bewilderment, unable to judge his mood accurately.

"You don't mind if I say I don't believe you and please will you stop? The others are coming!"

Humour deepened his voice, sardonic to the last. "Such a pity! You're either trying to frighten me off for my own good or malign me at every opportunity. As I see it, Perri, you like to live dangerously. It's no good and I can prove it's no good. I'll suffer insult and insolence from no woman, especially a honey-skinned brat!"

"Whatever you say, Mr. Faulkner!" She drew back from him a little, the silken mesh of her hair drawn back for the heat, glinting in the dappled sunlight. "I only want to help!"

"I'd never have guessed it!" There was a certain tartness in his voice that gave her pause.

"Sermons and symbolism," she said plaintively. "If it comes to that, you're a damned sight pricklier than I am. *And* unjust!"

"You're not taking me on, are you?" he asked in tones of the liveliest interest, blue eyes narrowing over her face.

"Only with the acutest misgivings. I know my limitations, if nothing else!"

"My dear child, just to please me?" His voice dropped to a soft drawl, moving into a new sphere of the senses. She was lost, lost, turning her brilliant, youthful face up to him, misliking the arrogant set of his head, that straight-down-the-nose look.

"I think not!" she said hardily.

"Be original at least. Don't let me have *all* my own way!"

She gazed back at him in mild consternation. He was teasing her, she knew *that*, yet there was a look on his lean, dark face she couldn't define or even recognize. The warm colour rushed to her face. "What woman could stop you?" she said sweetly. "You must have had an awfully exciting past!"

"You have my word on it!" His voice was sharp and amused. "But you knew that in the first instant!"

"Of course I did, but I'm damned well not going to provide you with a few more romantic interludes!"

He laughed out loud and flicked her cheek with his finger. "Only time will tell, pretty one!"

"You're impossible, aren't you?" She drew a quick, fortifying breath, filled with the reckless desire to say just about anything, her full, curving mouth tilting ironically.

"Careful, Perri!" he warned her. "I'm not entirely immune to all those sparkling little barbs!"

"But sometimes I can't resist them. It's useless,

146

though, isn't it? Like tilting at windmills. You'll never change!"

"Do you want me to?" He regarded her thoughtfully, black brows slanting quizzically.

For a moment she was struck into silence, her eyes flicking over his chiselled dark face, filled with a taunting diablerie. She swung her satiny, pale head, an odd excitement slipping through her veins.

"I won't answer that! All I *will* admit to is you have the most disconcerting effect upon me!"

"And I feel so damned guilty!"

"Bless you!" she said dryly, giving up the unequal struggle. "To think I was sitting here, enjoying the shade and minding my own business . . .!"

But she had lost him, his attention instantly diverted. His hand dropped to her shoulder, gripping, bruising, though she doubted he was aware of it, silencing her.

"Quiet now!" His dark head had shot up, his expression a compound of alertness and a no-nonsense concentration. The deeply blue gaze flickered about the clearing, listening, judging the quality of sound.

For no reason at all danger and doubt began to press down on her, communicated through his lean, strong hands.

"What is it?"

"Be still!"

Dandy, the little aboriginal stockboy, closed in, abandoning his mount, jerking his black curly head about with an uneasy twist. "Not such a good place, Boss! Plenty of truffles about in the brushwood. Wild pig, maybe!"

"You're probably right!" The blue eyes sharpened,

narrowing over the tangled undergrowth to the back of them. "Come on, we'll get going!"

Quite close by a bird started to sing with piercingly sweet intensity and Perri drew in her breath sharply, in bitter-sweet pleasure, the fine edge of sadness:

"Not while *I'm* still here, surely! Listen to that bird, it's a beautiful spot, Gray!"

He turned on her in devastating fashion, cutting right through her reverie, his hand on her arm, then he jerked his head about in mingled presentiment and fury as almost on cue, like some half expected nightmare, a wild boar, hideously ugly, ears flapping, tusks glinting, broke through the brushwood and charged towards Dandy, the nearest territorial invader.

For one startled instant, the aboriginal boy stood motionless, his chocolate brown face a study, then he veered, parrying frantically, fast, but not nearly fast enough, almost but not quite losing his head. Perri felt herself swaying in shock, the golden green glade a mass of dancing reflections. This couldn't be happening. It was too sudden, the progression from green peace to danger. Then she was lifted bodily clear of the ground, twisted high in the air and thrust forcibly on to the limb of a tree, her hair inextricably tangled in the leaves, gasping, the breath almost knocked out of her.

Faulkner's voice, harsh and urgent, split the air, reverberating around the wild bush.

"Jump, Dandy! Jump, damn it! Get a bloody move on, you fool!"

"Notta chance in hell, Boss!" The stockboy's voice crackled.

"...*now!*"

Dandy leapt like a great dancer, as much in instinctive obedience as the need for self-preservation, jack-knifing into the air, wiry legs spread, his gleaming eyes white-ringed with fright, while the boar, in a blind fury, ears flopping over its eyes, charged through the now open space, with remarkably little clearance, hurtling on for about a hundred yards in violent motion before wheeling to recharge, its great bulk of shoulder, neck and flank quivering.

There seemed no time to think of anything. The boy landed lightly enough, but one foot sank jarringly into a melon hole and buckled under him. He rolled and twisted on the grass, his sweating face registering pain, helpless with the certain expectation of being gored. Perri felt drained of all power to move or even scream. It was all her fault for being so stupidly stubborn. She clung to the branch with all the strength left in her, hearing the muffled throb of her heavily beating heart, not knowing what was to happen. Vaguely she saw a tall, powerful figure move with tigerish speed among the milling horses; the sun glinting off the long barrel of a rifle. Dandy was still lying on the ground, his twitching face ghastly in a mock grin, a tic convulsing his left cheek.

Oh, God! she thought desperately, her vision darkening. There was a metallic noise and she sucked in her breath, the sound of a rifle report cracking across the clearing.

The boar died within seconds of hitting its human target, the bullet taking it in the middle of the head, dropping it without so much as a drunken stagger. It let out one sickening, almost human keening squeal, then the blood burst from its head in a great crimson gout, thick and heavy, staining the grass.

Perri's stomach somersaulted, her hands started to shake uncontrollably, lost in a half world of impressions. She heard her uncle's shout of alarm, but the situation was totally impossible. She couldn't bear it a minute longer. All that blood! She was slipping, falling, the ground in her crazy path, very close, very solid, a green wilderness, then she passed out, coming to rest on the coarse, thick grass, lying quite peacefully, long fragile bones, breakable looking, one arm outflung, the fingers of the other hand half curled into her palm, her face the colour of porcelain.

Faulkner reached her first, closing the short distance between them, dropping to his knees, on his dark face a catalyst of emotions, anger predominant!

It was ten o'clock. A pale moon shone over the garden, casting long shadows down the arches of the trees and illuminating the little marble dryad that guarded the lily pool. Perri stood for a moment in the soft brilliance, a bitter-sweet nostalgia tugging at her heart. The silent dryad seemed to study her compassionately, her lovely limbs extended towards the sparkling, lily-strewn water, the deeply moulded mouth, faintly smiling. Perri walked towards her, her whispery voice gentle, directed at the palely gleaming figure:

"What are *you* smiling at? Life's more complicated than that!"

The smiling nymph didn't answer, wonderfully serene,

and Perri sank down on the garden seat, staring pensively about her. The peace and quiet of the place was remarkable, the night air warm and sweet with the incomparable scents of the garden, some fragrant shrub with the combined perfume of jasmine and orange blossom. A faint spirit-wind stroked the silver sheet of water, creating shadowy ripples, rustling the ornamental grasses that flanked the pool. Nearly all sound was made by the wind, all merging into one song, quiet and deep.

Perri's face softened and saddened. Whatever happened she had these moments on Coorain to remember. She blinked back quick emotional tears, her eyes enormous with a hint of strain and temperament. All through dinner, Gray had treated her to a formidable, superb courtesy as remote as the next world, concealing, at best, that he was sick of the sight of her, her silly adolescent behaviour. It had been hard to believe, meeting his blue, indifferent gaze, that he had ever for an instant been attracted to her. She had been fighting a losing game all along. The events of the afternoon had shown her up, found the chink in her armour. She was a city girl pampered and ornamental, hopelessly inadequate when it came to fending for herself, outside of the cushioned, urban habitat.

Lorna Talbot had implied as much without using a single word, trading heavily on her own undeniable competence. She and her daughter were, quite simply, countrywomen, steady and reliable, tried and tested under stress of all kinds. Perri, the interloper, had been added up sum total and found wanting. It was ludicrously unexpected in the Outback to faint at the first sign of blood, fall out of trees and raise a lump on one's skull. Perri fingered her sore head gingerly, her skin still white-petalled with shock.

Right through the long meal, the twin yellow gaze of Kim and her mother, unreasonably smug, hadn't spared her, raking over her constantly, informing her plainly that she was no good at all the way she was and the sooner she got back to her own way of life the better. Perri smiled a little grimly, oddly defensive. She was no more than a passing acquaintance, "ships that pass in the night and speak to each other. . . ." No one on Coorain could ever learn to take her seriously. She couldn't even ride well, an effortless accomplishment for all of them, let alone shoot or cut out cattle. Only her own, her uncle and Mark, had regarded her with concern, her heightened air of fragility, forcing home on her the terrible responsibility of appearing normal; contenting herself with the occasional witty interjection, endeavouring to pass off the whole situation with a light, self-deprecatory laugh. What more could they expect from a city girl?

It was a matter of pride. And she had *that*, though in private she dealt with herself severely. She longed to ask Gray what he really thought of her and risk the consequences, but never, never could she summon up the nerve. Probably he would let her down lightly. He wasn't the type to relish pulling wings off butterflies, and that was what she was; a gauzy, ineffectual butterfly when it came to the more serious rigours of the back country. She couldn't ask any special favours. The pattern was all too familiar. She had based her impetuous love for him on a faulty premise, for apart from the odd spasm

152

of sexual attraction, her feelings were not returned. He had looked at her and judged her with a swift gathering of all his resources, finding she still baffled him but definitely did not intrigue him.

The swift lick of humiliation brought her right back to her senses. She shivered and her heart contracted with a nervousness as real as it was absurd. It was only beating at half strength anyway. It was a never-ending pity she had become involved at all. It would take her years and years to get over Gray Faulkner, if she ever got over him at all.

"A pity beyond all telling is hid in the heart of love!" A fragment of Yeats came to her and she said it aloud, bending her head, for it was her own face she was hiding. A dark shadow loomed suddenly behind her, soundless, with a marvellous economy of movement, the voice black velvet, smoothly humouring her.

"I do beg your pardon, but you haven't taken to talking to yourself?"

Perri spun her head defiantly, willing herself not to succumb. "Damn it!" she said clearly. "It would be you!"

He paused, looking down at her, his lean hands gripping the back of the seat. "You've done it, Perri. You've done it again! I must give credit where credit is due!"

"You don't as a rule!" she said recklessly, then stiffened intuitively as he reached over and grasped her arm, twisting her to her feet. His fingers fell to her wrist.

"What, no pulse? My poor fool of a child, you appear to have died in the last five minutes!"

"A pulse is no test," she said sweetly, trying in vain to

153

break his grip. "Don't try and twist my heart for me, Gray Faulkner!"

"And *could* I?"

"Yes, indeed! Top of the list!" she said tauntingly. "Is that the answer you need? I've said all along you wouldn't make a good loser!"

"That does it!" His hand tangled in her hair, trailing it around her throat, tightening a little.

"Don't worry, in another week or so I'll be gone!" she said breathlessly, swaying under his hands. It was appalling the power he had over her.

"Must you?" A crooked smile played about his mouth. "I've never been so disappointed in my life!"

"That's likely! Let me go, Gray, I never make a fool of myself more than once in the same day!"

"A bit risky, I'll admit," he agreed coolly. "But never mind, little one, no one is perfect. Very few women, indeed, would be so frank about their own deficiencies!"

Her eyes flicked his arrogant, dark face, stung by his tone. "I'm coming to hate you!" she said warningly.

"That's a bit strong! And I really don't see why you're whispering. If you were any sort of a woman, you'd stay and see I get my deserts. Come hell and high water, as the saying goes!"

"That's the whole bit, I *can't*! Something fatal would happen!"

He laughed and for a moment she thought she would hit him, then she weakened, shaking her head rather helplessly.

"Well, at least I provide you with some amusement!"

"You do that, Perri. Either you're not quite normal,

or in a bad state of nerves. Let's try and look at this like two adults, consoling each other. I'm prepared to face each problem as it comes. For one thing, I'd never let you handle a gun. Much too distracting for one's peace of mind, and I'd like to see a great deal more of this world!"

He laughed gently, a faintly clandescent sound, and her eyes went iridescent with a trace of tears.

"Thanks for the whole chain of compliments!"

He shook her a little, his voice very cool and tantalising. "Try and look at it more positively, my lamb. This afternoon, you were hopeless! Not unpleasing to look at, flaked out on the grass, but hopeless: Small, beaten, too vulnerable by half! Of course, in some ways you're quite intelligent!"

"In others ... pretty rotten! Thanks for spelling it out. Now I know!" She looked up at him briefly, very tall, broad-shouldered, vividly handsome. The words came out in a strange little torment. "I love you, Gray Faulkner. I always knew I would. Now I do. You're a poisonous man!"

"Who's going to call your bluff, pretty one!" His eyes, flame blue, licked over her. "It's remarkable you've escaped me so far. No, don't tremble, this is a private, not a public scandal. What's so sinister about that? You've got nothing to be afraid of! This is just the day for excitements!"

"Please, Gray!" She tilted her head back, arching her spine, trying to size up her chances.

"*Please, Gray!*" he mocked her tremulous tone, his lean hands strangely deliberate. "Now shut up! That way

155

it will be less difficult. It must have leapt to your eye right from the first minute that I found you irresistible, though we might never understand each other!"

A shiver broke through her. The face she turned up to him was as pale as a flower, almost ethereal with a shimmery, slanting gaze that would stop any man. He laughed in his throat, sharply satirical, but all that she heard was the slow pounding of the blood in her head, the echo of her heart. Nothing before him or after him existed. It might have been the end of the world coming, or a few moments of radiant annihilation.

Hands caught her and her breath stopped. She turned up her mouth in a blind yearning and he claimed it with a sensual abandonment that swept everything before it, so that somehow they merged, the one to the other; silver and èbony, as indivisible as the dark rushing night and the luminous moonlight. The veil of her lashes shifted and came down, a circle of flame where her heart had been, the immediate world remote.

Beneath his mouth he felt her soft lips quiver in what might have been a soft moan, but he continued to kiss her, pressing her head back into the hard curve of his shoulder, slowing and lengthening those moments of shattering sensation, arousing in her a knife-edged response, controlling her with a single-minded determination and command, tasting the wild, sweet flavour of her mouth. Whatever else he could reject, it wasn't her physical reality, the profound mystery of her femininity, that could throw him into a turmoil of the senses. If it wasn't love that consumed them, changed them, drew them inexorably together, it was some violent emotion, tumultuous and shaking that one, at least, refused to recognise.

When he finally released her, she kept her eyes shut, her skin hot and feverish, her head aching with a kind of frustrated passion. Her hair had fallen loose in a silver quill over her shoulder, and he put out a hand in pretended contrition, smoothing it back behind her ears.

"Poor harried child!" he said in a dark, unsettling voice. "What have I done to you?"

She did not answer but opened her eyes, gleaming like ice crystals. If she expected to see tenderness on his dark face, there was no sign of it, no sign of the frantic emotions such as she had experienced, only a sardonic control, faintly saturnine.

"You're not human at all!" she said wonderingly, her voice charged with the primitive desire to hurt him; a desire all the more intense because she loved him.

A strange expression crossed his face, glittered into his eyes, flashing formidably.

"Then what *am* I, you perverse little witch? You make no sense at all!"

She stopped abruptly at the hard edge in his voice, clenching her hands together, her knees weak and uncertain. She dared not fling another remark at him. Whatever she had said, it had been the wrong thing. He stood motionless, his brilliant gaze downbent, yet there was a curious tension about him, a coiled alertness, that sent a thrill of near fear along her spine.

He shrugged, his tone cynical, seeing her surrender.

"So! I can hardly believe it! You're learning a little sense. Even *you* can be appalled by your own audacity. You wanted me to kiss you – I did. But don't worry, you

157

can trust in my discretion. Even my worst enemy, which just could turn out to be you, couldn't call me a gossip!"

His eyes were so brilliant, she felt like shielding her face from them, his expression dark and immobile. A shiver started at her nape and she made a futile attempt to defend herself.

"You completely misjudge me!" she said swiftly, turning up a face fragile and delicate in the moonlight, her eyes glowing feverishly.

He responded with the deepest irony, his face as arrogant as the devil, ruthless even, tempered steel. "Your behaviour is *odd*, you'll admit," he said wearily. "In fact, I don't know how we'll bear to part with you. So unusual. So many surprises. And beautiful too! I'm afraid, Perri, you're just too good to be true!"

"No, I have a headache, that's all!" She looked back at him helplessly, almost desperate to escape him. She sounded as mournful as a small girl with the tears, deep and irresistible, not too far off. She rubbed a hand over her mouth in instinctive hunger and he suddenly relented, his eyes losing their cold glitter.

"Oh, what's the use!" he said briefly, his voice implacably hard. "I feel pretty grim myself. You're nothing but a silver-headed daisy with a mild case of hysteria. Come up to the house. Have a drink! Curb your mad, adolescent mind! I've a good mind to stick with you, Perri. Challenge - that's all that matters to me!"

Perri, dazed but willing, went with him. He seemed utterly fed up. A devil roused in him. She said nothing, but her white throat throbbed. Oh, to be a man! So careless and uncaring! What a fool she was, squandering all her emotions. There was no tenderness in him, no real feeling for her. She drew a soft, shuddery breath and he suddenly bent his head in a kind of expert, impatient passion, catching the point of her chin, and dropping a hard kiss on her pulsing, red mouth. One small blind instant of pleasure and pain.

"Poor Perri!" he said brutally. "Pay up and like it! You put me in a misery of rage, but suddenly I can see what's wrong with you. No woman is incalculable! I intend to fathom you out!"

Her hand moved in his convulsively and his grip tightened a fine flare to his nostrils. "No, it's not a bit of good struggling! One of these days I'm going to catch up with you. Maybe the day after tomorrow. I'll make damn sure of that! It's never too late to teach you a much-needed lesson!"

"No, I suppose not!" she said, raising her head almost fearfully to his autocratic dark face, "but that kind of thing needs co-operation, surely?"

"For God's sake!" he said grimly. "Not another word! For your misdeeds, you'll see the rest of your stay out. That's the way it is, I'm afraid!"

A pulse began to hammer painfully in Perri's throat. She moved her lips faintly, stifling a soft cry. She loved him and he was playing some game of his own, with the game almost won. It was not to be borne! Desolation a thousand times over. She felt like running on ahead, but he wouldn't allow that, using his strength to reduce her futile little movements to impotence. She could see that she was shaking his self-control but she could never override him.

She sobered abruptly, walking beside him in quiet resignation, turning the other cheek, unprotesting, her shining head near his shoulder. A myriad delirious plans rushed through her head. Without position and power, a man like Gray Faulkner couldn't find happiness. There seemed no real place in his life for love. That lovely myth! That legend! Only women needed love or the illusion of it to find fulfilment, and women were so easily discarded. From now on she had no choice. Better the ground open up and devour her than she persist in her dreams without substance. Only a fool built on fantasy, and she wasn't *that* yet! But into her bewildered and passionate mind came the thought of the rest of her life: A progression of empty rooms, one after the other. The sight and the sound of him nowhere! Pain began to bite at the edges of her pride. She loved him, and she had no other desire in her whole traitorous heart!

CHAPTER VII

FOR three long days Perri flung herself into her work so that by the end of the third day she was filled with exhaustion, retiring early on the pretext of writing a batch of long-overdue letters. Up in her bedroom, she switched on the dressing table light, seeing the room reflected in the mirror, softly glimmering; a pale wall-to-wall carpet in tone-on-tone golds, melons and pumpkins and celadon, graceful heirloom furniture, an elegant striped paper, a sunburst gilt mirror, a few beautiful landscapes arranged in perfect balance, a Victorian sofa, upholstered in silk damask, a writing desk and a carved chair, a Queen Anne cabinet crammed with a collection of porcelain sculptures.

She dropped her head slightly so that she was left staring at a little Nepalese Buddha that sat on the dressing table, its hands in the position of Giving and Teaching. She couldn't think why, but the sight of it made her feel mortally wounded, swept into a limbo of desolation, becalmed, lost. Gray had once told her the little figure was a valuable antique, dating back to the late sixteenth century, the expression in his eyes calm but possessive, illuminated by his love for his home and its beautiful contents; a kind of dynamic inner intensity. Nothing in Coorain homestead was locked away, hoarded up in cabinets. Everything was out on display, to be seen and admired, touched with loving fingers.

In the glimmering light, Perri could almost make out a tall, lean figure behind her. She knew the exact mould and expression on his dark, handsome face, the garnet blue eyes. Probably he was counting up the days and the hours and the minutes until she was gone. The simple effort of being civil to her was showing, a cool glitter in his eyes when he spoke to her, steel in his voice. She couldn't live under the same roof and not be aware of it. She was no more than a pretty invader, a hundred per cent out of place in the Heartland, the eerie desert atmosphere into which she had been plunged. Her eyes, misted with tears met her own reflection, slid away full of confusions and heartaches. She could almost wish she had never laid eyes on him. She had been happy before in her contented small world; now . . . *this*!

There was a knock on the door and she felt the first brush of apprehension, her mind and body clenching together. For a moment she stood motionless, breathing constricted air, then the tap came again, firming with resolution. Perri released her breath slowly, blinked away the slight glaze in her eyes and walked across the carpet, bracing herself with the simple gesture of opening the door. Her head jerked upwards and she stood silent and appalled, hoping none of her feelings were showing on her face.

Lorna Talbot smiled and moved past her, queenly

cool, guarding her own thoughts, her yellow cat's eyes denying the charming consideration in her voice.

"Forgive me for disturbing you, my dear, but you seemed tired and rather dispirited at dinner. Is there anything I could get you?"

She didn't wait for an answer but brushed past Perri with long, gliding steps, standing at ease in the centre of the room, checking its appointments as though she half expected to find at least one valuable object missing. Reassured but not entirely satisfied, the bright, searching gaze swept back to Perri's young face, indecision haunting the wide, tilted eyes.

"It must be very difficult for you, I know!" The words came almost caressingly as though they were relished and Perri swung her pale, shining head in a stupor of shock with the certain premonition of what was to come.

Carry the fight into the enemy's camp! she thought dismally, stalling for time.

"I'm sorry, but I'm not with you, Mrs. Talbot. I shouldn't be a bit surprised if I miss the rest of it as well!"

"Oh, but you *are*, my dear!" Lorna Talbot said instantly, her firm voice infinitely self-assured. "You see, I know your little secret. Does that surprise you? It shouldn't! The young are so very easy to read. From the first moment you arrived on Coorain, your feelings have been as blatant as a radio announcement, brutal even. They've reached us all. You really are naïve, aren't you? Wrapped in your cocoon of illusion, the apex of imbecility you young girls seem to indulge in!"

Perri stared back at her almost hynotically. She could

163

detect in herself rising anger, but she was powerless to control it. "In all my born days I've never struck anyone like you, Mrs. Talbot," she said candidly. "You've always disliked me, haven't you?"

"Disliked?" Lorna Talbot frowned, savouring the word and finding it wanting. "My dear girl, I've no feelings for you one way or the other. At the same time I feel it my duty to save *you* needless self-injury, and the rest of us embarrassment. You're only days away from leaving Coorain. Why jeopardise a pleasant and enormously beneficial visit? Your unhappiness is being remarked by everyone!"

"No, really!" Perri said lightly. "I rather suspect you've enjoyed it. In fact, you probably started it!"

"Started what?" the sharply tolerant voice asked calmly. "Don't be so obtuse. A child could work it out. You're feeling cheated, betrayed. You fell violently in love and heaven knows no one could blame you, but you must admit you knew the name of the game and that's all it was! Just a pleasantly meaningless diversion to fill in the time. Men are like that, especially the wildly attractive ones. It's just something we women have to accept. Of course in one respect you've been cheated as all women are at some stage of their lives, and I feel sorry for you. But pride is your strongest weapon. It may seem a little old-fashioned, a marriage of convenience, but Gray and my daughter are ideally suited. You must have remarked on that in some of your close private discussions with that objectionable young colleague of yours. Gray and Kim share the same background, the same interests. They have a deep respect for one another and a

164

biding affection. Whatever Gray felt for you, it was physical attraction at its lowest level. Some men are particularly vulnerable to blonde charms! Oh, I'm sorry, my dear, I've hurt you, and I'm deeply sorry!"

Perri smiled a little, grimly amused. "You haven't hurt me exactly, Mrs. Talbot. Disgusted me might be closer the mark. Vindictiveness in a woman is an insupportable handicap. The thing is, whether you're right or you're wrong, it's none of your business. I don't believe Gray *will* marry Kim, though I can't deny she'd make a perfect helpmate. Perhaps you'd be wise to dispense with some of your own blindness!"

Lorna Talbot's dark arching brows almost shot away to her hairline. "It's not important what you believe!" she pointed out, coldly inflexible. "One day soon, you'll read in the society pages just how wrong you've been. By then maybe your own little disaster won't seem so important. You're a pretty girl in a style I don't admire. A bit obvious, perhaps! Back in the city, I'm sure you'll find plenty of suitable boy-friends. You simply haven't the capacity to stand up to life out here. Believe me, my dear, it's high time you and I had this little chat, though I don't expect you to appreciate it now. Naturally I'll give you my unstinting support to get through the remaining time. If you try to act normally, I'm sure you'll earn Gray's undying gratitude. You can't imagine how many young women have made fools of themselves over him. Terribly wearing! In fact, I'm even tempted to tell you how many for your own good. But of course, at your age, you can't be expected to know what a man like Gray Faulkner would want in a woman – correction, a wife!

Just take my word for it, it's no one like you! I shudder at the thought. I'm by way of being an expert in these things. Besides, Gray has confided in me on one or two occasions. He respects my judgment!"

"I don't wonder!" Perri said instantly. "It would prove much easier in the long run!"

Surprisingly Lorna Talbot flushed, her voice unexpectedly disconcerted, snappish even. "My dear girl!" she said tersely, "my sole interest at the moment is helping you over a difficult spot. Men have always exploited women shamelessly for their own ends. Gray is devastatingly attractive – too much so for an uneventful life. In actual fact, it was a once-in-a-lifetime opportunity for you to have met him at all, or been a guest on Coorain!"

Perri looked sardonically into the glittering eyes, glassy with dislike.

"Mrs. Talbot," she said evenly, "your simple good-heartedness is quite beyond me. I don't know what to say, unless it's remarkable that you've escaped your reward!"

"An excellent idea!" the older woman said virtuously, with a rapid waning of that unfamiliar colour. "I prayed this situation wouldn't arise, but it has. Sometimes it's necessary to be cruel to be kind. My advice to you, young woman, for what it's worth: from now on, disregard Gray. Your whole future is locked to it. You can only get hurt, perhaps irreparably so. I realise the young like exploiting new areas of pain, but if you follow my advice, you'll save yourself a great deal of embarrassment – not to mention the rest of us!"

"So early in the game too," Perri observed ironically. "Before it actually got going!"

"Another thing to remember, miss! Kim has been very forbearing about it all – this outsize crush of yours! In my young days I would never have stood for it!"

"Would you mind leaving, Mrs. Talbot? *Now!* I don't feel I can find adequate polite responses to all your kindnesses. Not at this rate, anyhow!"

"Are you sure you're all right?" Lorna Talbot insisted, frankly malicious. "You don't look well!"

"If you go *now*," Perri said quietly, a wry sense of humour coming to her rescue, "I promise not to open my mouth until you've gone through the door. I'm as full of faults as the next one, I might just run off the rails, start a brawl – anything!"

"But I'm helping you, my dear. You should be grateful!"

"Oh, but I *am*! Put an end to all these triflings, Mrs. Talbot. You're most exhilarating company, as I'm sure you've been told before. In fact, I'll go one step further and say I'll never forget you. Kim is lucky indeed to have such a masterful mother!"

This time the thrust went home. Lorna Talbot's face sharpened, her long narrow mouth assuming a bitter twist.

"Did that make you feel any better?"

"I must admit it did!" Perri broke the strained and painful silence. "I warned you I can be as bitchy as the next one. Though you started first. It's time you were making a move, Mrs. Talbot. The only gift I crave is a good sleep!"

"In that case, we might have a happy ending, after all. Good night, my dear. You must be able to take your medicine. That's the way by which we're all judged!"

Perri walked to the door and held it. "May you have a similiar chance at glory, Mrs. Talbot, though I doubt it. Your ambitions, I know, are all for your daughter. Don't allow yourself to be daunted by their grandeur!"

Lorna Talbot waved a nonchalant hand, her eyes narrowing over the faked calm in Perri's pale face. "Say what you like, my dear. I can see how you *feel*. No one can accuse me of dereliction of duty. If you disregard my advice, you're quite free to enjoy your own funeral. It doesn't matter a damn to me. I'm sure the experience will be rewarding, no matter how it turns out!" She turned away abruptly, having played her hand, and Perri shut the door, the shock to her system so complete she couldn't fight back. She wheeled away to the bed and flung herself on it, clouds of humiliation and unhappiness descending on her head, stunning her to such a degree that she couldn't get up when a second summons came to her door, though she managed a weak: "Come in!"

Mark popped his head around the door, at the sight of her helpless abandon, too astonished to speak.

"What was *that* all about?" he asked finally, almost tiptoeing into the room. "I just saw Lucrezia leaving!"

Perri turned her head, muttering faintly: "Nothing! She just wanted to know what I wanted for my breakfast!"

It was such an absurd lie, Mark gave an odd little chortle. "Well, I can see asking you any more questions would be a sheer waste of breath. But something is going on. She wasn't trying to chat you up, was she, the old vixen? I know what women are like. Ghastly!"

The affection and sympathy in his voice plucked at chords of self-pity Perri didn't want to own. She made a great effort to return to dignity and calm, Mark's eyes fixed with great penetration on her face.

"Shall I tell you something, sweetie?" he said brusquely. "I can't wait until we're off Coorain. It's been marvellous in lots of ways and it will spread Prof's fame, but it's made you unhappy. You're mad about Faulkner. Cooked your goose in that way. Don't bother to deny it. Everything about you screams it from the rooftops. A lunatic love affair!"

"So I've been told!" Perri cried mournfully, the room blurring under the swift onrush of tears.

"I'll killl him!" Mark shouted, pacing the room furiously.

"You're not old enough!"

Mark jerked to a halt, thinking that over. He clenched his hands, the light of rage in his eyes. "An alternative and safer solution would be to arrange some kind of bizarre accident. That sort of thing is always happening out here!"

Perri sat up abruptly, her ash-gold hair spilling wildly about her flushed face and over-bright eyes. "The solemn truth, my vengeful school friend, if you want it, is this: he never encouraged me, not in the least. I forget just what happened. All I know is it's like falling under a train, crushed to pulp!"

"Oh, for heaven's sake, girl," Mark burst out wrathfully, "where's your sense of humour? You're only moping. You'll get over it. Back home you'll go sour on the whole deal. The trouble with Faulkner is he's dynamite.

169

All that filthy power and position, and sex appeal too. It's indecent, not to speak of undemocratic. In fact to a donkey like me it's vaguely unbelievable. The funny part is that really dashing types like Faulkner often finish up with the weirdest women – frigid usually, fat, frumpy, faces like horses. Remember that Max Drynan, the lecturer? His wife rated a suicide leap. But she suited him. They seemed happy enough. There's no telling what a man will settle for!"

"Actually I *have* been told!" Perri pointed out a little hysterically, waylaid by all the red herrings, her eyes great glistening lakes.

"Oh, I *see*! said the blind man!" Mark murmured bitterly, his tirade coming to a whistling stop. "Well, you must admit the girl has got sterling characteristics not often found in most of us!" His black eyes had gone blank, his voice expressionless. "We're out of place here, sweetie, that's what it is. In which case, we'd better beat the hell home before any more heartbreak besets us!" He advanced a step, some new intelligence coming into his face. "I'm nevertheless inclined to think it's a put-up job! I can personally, off my own bat, vouch for the fact that Kim Talbot has never been in love with anyone. Hero-worship isn't at all the same thing. Her dear, dreadful mother has actually engineered this whole atrocity. She's the type to take pleasure in inflicting pain, though far be it from me to cast discredit on anyone. Come on, Perri, sharpen yourself up! You're the picture of inconsolable grief. The little mermaid bereft!"

"Well, naturally!" she said in a muffled-up voice. "But don't worry! I'll pull myself together, never fear.

170

No special privileges allowed here! "

Mark made one of his odd, in-character sounds. "It's not going to be a love-hate now, is it? That's extremely dangerous in a woman, so I've been told! "

Perri was torn between laughter and tears. Her hands dropped to her sides and she turned her face to look at him. "It's silly to keep you in suspense a minute longer. For some reason that seems inexplicable now, I'm exhausted of all emotion. There will be no outbursts of primitive passion this trip. I think I might justly claim to have only a splitting headache! "

"Poor little thing! " Mark came round the end of the bed and patted her shoulder. "I loathe that woman to the depths of her shallow soul! "

"Mark dear," she said, comforted, "that's not manly! You can't really blame her for wishing us out of the way. God knows I *want* to go! "

"I find that highly improbable! " he pointed out dryly.

"My friend! "

For a moment the two looked at each other speechlessly, then Mark spoke with forced lightness trying to break the pathos of the moment, the nostalgia of long years of close friendship, with humour. "As a connoisseur of scenes, I shall treasure this one. Whatever I can do to help, my lady, I will. In the days gone past I would have thrown down my coat for you to tread upon. If you want to pack, we can leave by the next train! "

Perri laughed as he meant her to. She laughed for a long time, the tears sliding weakly down her young, satiny cheeks. Mark looked on with mingled love and pity. "I'm glad you're feeling happy again! " he said gently. "Get a good night's sleep and I'll see you in the morning. Try and think of what my dad always says: worse things have happened at sea! It helps! "

But of course it didn't! Perri cried herself to sleep that night with the passion and abandon that only the young are capable of.

It was very quiet in the library, all sound muffled by book-covered walls, set in arcaded recesses. The Professor, head bent, was engrossed in a series of reproductions of sorcery figures drawn on the walls of one of the rock shelters, examining them carefully with complete absorption. Several were of women, presumably unfaithful wives, who had been punished by drawing their likeness, which was then sung over until the unfaithful one sickened and died. Others were male figures, the lovers, perhaps, who unquestionably had suffered the same fate.

Perri occupied herself with copying out two long love cycles, specifying the meaning of each word separately. Today her job was just a job. She met it with no interest, no scientific attitude, no real sense of responsibility. On Coorain, she thought cynically, there were many representations of love magic; drawings of the desired ones on the walls of the sandstone caves. The old love formulas were used by men as well as women, practised all over the continent. If only she had the power to draw one of purely magical intent designed to draw the loved one closer! She drew a deep, shaky breath and began to doodle on a blank sheet in front of her.

Her uncle looked up with an expression, half concern, half resignation.

"That was a particularly pathetic sigh! I've been pushing you too hard. You've fallen down on the job. What the devil is that? Doodling, wishful thinking? A characteristic failing in women, even the best of them! You're thinner than you used to be, pet. We won't be able to find you next. Why don't you go out for a while? Get a breath of fresh air. I can carry on here. I want to see if I can trace some of those old revenge expeditions. Those little pearl-shaped discs Mark found are definitely death charms. Gray gave me a lead on the painted stones. He's been absolutely marvellous, hasn't he? None of us will ever be able to thank him enough!"

"That wanted saying!" Perri murmured intensely. "He actually deserves to be knighted!" She stood up and clutched at the back of her chair like a woman suffering from vertigo.

The Professor smiled with startling sweetness. "If it was in my power, I'd insist on it!" he exclaimed, turning with real relish to an interesting brass rubbing of a spirit figure with an eagle hawk head and multiple arms.

"Yoho!" he said happily. "This alone could be the subject of a paper!"

Perri looked across at him with a rush of pride and a certain wry amusement. This is the real justification for the trip, she thought without disillusionment. Professor Lucas B. Greenwood in his Utopia ... Coorain; with sketches, rubbings, photographs and documents, the material for an erudite report from one of the country's most highly respected anthropologists. She could see by his heavy, handsome face that he felt in great form, thoroughly happy, immersed in that all-important thing

... his work, his life interest. She looked a little moodily around the room, her eyes lighting on the lovely veneer of the old cedar furniture. There was a sense of continuity about the house that pervaded the atmosphere. One family that had set out to make the house as beautiful, as comfortable and as welcoming as possible. Curious, but she had never experienced that feeling before. Never in any of the striking contemporary homes she had been in for all their luxurious appointments.

Her lower lip was trembling slightly and she bit on it, unhappy at the way she was coping with an emotional crisis. In another minute her eyes would fill with tears. Love affairs were notoriously tricky, one-sided ones a tragedy. There might be more heartbreak to come before the trip was over. The Professor had his head turned away with a slight frown.

"I've cross-checked a few of Mark's reports and I'm pleased to say I can't catch him out, though the style is rather pure and cold for such fascinating material. Still," he looked up and smiled, "Mark likes to express himself in sober, scientific terms, and nothing wrong with that! A more vivid impression would still have been as convincing. I'll speak to him about it!" He looked at his niece with his fine grey eyes. "Have you finished those songs yet?"

"Only one!"

"Well, put it in the box, then!" He squinted down at it. "Good girl, that's beautifully neat. First class, always providing it doesn't turn out to be nonsense. A most orderly mind, in my golden opinion. We'll soon have you an old hand at the game even if your heart's not in it!"

He hesitated, longing to see Perri's illuminating smile, but she looked rather sad, forlorn even.

"I say!" he said with real concern flinging down his glasses. "You're pale! It must be a head coming on, as my dear secretary is wont to say. For God's sake go out and nip it in the bud. What do you say? Come on, child, a suggestion of that nature usually requires comment!"

Perri blinked her thick, silky lashes. "I'm sorry, Uncle Luke. I'm daydreaming, I think. I will go out. Do you mind?"

"Of course not, dear!" said Greenwood. "I should say it would be in your best interests. Now where is Mark?" he added almost awkwardly. "It's a pretty rotten state of affairs when a member of my team can't be punctual. Unpunctuality is the sign of a disorganised mind!"

"Thanks for the compliment!" Mark announced breezily, appearing in the open doorway, his footsteps inaudible on the thick carpet.

The Professor turned and looked at him. "Well, I'll be damned! That's quite all right, my boy, no favouritism allowed! To be honest, I did think you'd show up, give or take an hour. Devoted to your job, I know!"

"Stop being nice about it!" Mark said cheerfully, advancing on them with buoyant paces. "You're past forgiveness in any case, Prof!"

"That may well be, but we still have work to be processed!" The Professor turned to his niece with a gentle aside. "Perri, my dear, you may go. Mark is in charge now, or he thinks he is. Take the day off!"

"That's a good idea!" Mark seconded, looking at Perri thoughtfully. "Go down to the yards. They're breaking in the range-bred horses. Pretty exciting! That's why I was late!"

"With all humbleness," the Professor said sarcastically, "what am I going to do about this chap? Chitter, chatter and so on!"

"You're just selfish!" Mark said reproachfully.

"I'm off!" Perri intervened, moving quickly and speaking over her shoulder.

"That's just as well!" The Professor nodded encouragement and Perri walked to the door, closing it softly behind her, hearing a protest of Mark's being overridden by her uncle's authoritative voice as "gross oversimplification!" She smiled to herself, only a little ironically, knowing herself to be easily dismissable. There was no doubt about it, men really were different, not given to headaches and heartaches and nervous prostrations. The breeze in the hallway was like a healing spirit. She put a hand to her forehead, then walked up the beautiful main staircase and along the gallery with a kind of desperate urgency, disquiet in her luminous grey eyes. In her bedroom, she changed her dress for a cotton shirt and slacks, her depression deepening slowly, irresistibly. She didn't feel in the least like seeing the wild horses broken in, all that great rearing pride, the flashing spirit and independence systematically silted away. It was bad enough having her own wild urges curbed. She would spend the day in the hill country, visit her favourite rock pool, where Time began . . . if she could ever find it again. She thrust out her slender, tapering fingers and touched the little Buddha, then left the room, shutting the door softly.

At the end of the gallery her attention was caught as ever by the first in the line of family portraits. John Gray Faulkner looked down from his gilded frame, dark and handsome and dashing indeed. A vital, forceful man with vision and the practical qualities to realise a dream. Years and years from now, she would be able to draw a picture of that notable face – the eyes, the high cheek-bones, the lines from nose to mouth, the sweep of thick dark hair. The resemblance to Gray was remarkable, like some mysterious revelation, some curious magic.

Her smouldering eyes savoured the portrait, fighting the temptation to touch it, trace the curve of that sensual, sensitive mouth. A tapestry chair, a delightful contrast, stood just to the right of the portrait. Perri considered sinking into it with a settled air of permanency. She loved this place, and what was more melancholy, she was be-devilled by its owner. Her eyes glittered suddenly, but she clung to her resolution blinking the brightness of loss and humiliation away. Nothing like Gray Faulkner would ever happen to her again. Perhaps in time she would find it all a waking dream.

The portrait disturbed her with the curious unsettling familiarity. She fell to noticing little differences.

"I suppose that's as good a way as any of passing the time?"

The voice was directly behind her, guarded and enig-matic, but the same black magic. Because she could not speak, Perri swung her blonde head, forcing herself to look into his dark face and meet the quicksilver flash of his eyes.

"So you won't answer?" His voice turned amused,

mocking, complicated.

"I *can't*!" She dropped her lids, her eyes almost tragically despairing, then she tried to move past him.

He gave the impression of not moving, yet he had her, compelling her back along the hallway.

"I hardly see you at all, Perri! So why go?"

Waves of quivering excitement were breaking over her. She was also conscious of a kind of secret shame. This power he had over her! His expression was mocking, but she could feel an answering tension in him. She realised now, with a kind of chronic fatalism, that she had fallen in love with him on sight. It could and did happen in life as well as in novels. Her eyes were the colour of smoke, fixed on him in a strange fascination.

"You don't give much away, do you?" he asked, and touched her cheek lightly, a shivery caress.

"I'm going out, Gray!" she said in a soft, agitated voice, her beautiful hair falling loose.

"Are you telling me, or pleading to be let go?"

"You know the answer to that one," she said painfully.

"*Do* I? Nothing in the whole of creation is darker or more incomprehensible than a woman's mind!"

"Nevertheless you're safe with me!" she burst out recklessly, just to satisfy a foolish urge.

He laughed under his breath. "I never feel safe alone with any woman!"

"Why not?" she challenged him. "Nothing is going to happen here. No furtive intrigue!"

His eyes flashed, some intense disturbance in his dark, stormy face. "You *are* a fool!" he said forcibly, his anger like a physical force that vibrated between them, sending reverberations right down to her being. Then all at once it was something different, overwhelming in its utter completeness; his mouth on hers like a fierce, elemental impulse, kissing her with a frightening insistence, like a deliberate attempt at seduction.

She tried to push him away, frightened by her own sensations, but his hand slid under her chin to hold her head fast.

"No, my love, don't struggle. It's high time you and I came to a reckoning!"

The vital warmth was in his voice again, melting away all her resolutions. She closed her eyes and turned up her mouth, her pride shattered . . . a small price. He was like nobody else, a magnetic force that drew her beyond all thought of the consequences. When it was all over, she would have to cope with the shipwreck she had made for herself. But not now . . . not now . . . with the world dissolving in a dark golden haze.

His hands held her shoulders. He was looking straight at her with his beautiful, vivid eyes, his glance moving lightly over her heightened beauty, the fine-drawn perfection of intense emotion. Perri waited for him to speak, not knowing quite what to expect, and he gave a brief laugh that seemed to hold the same lick of triumph that glittered from his eyes.

"You answered me, Perri, in my own language. For once in your life admit it!"

She could feel herself go rigid with a kind of stunned bewilderment. It took a lot of courage to say what she did, but he had broken through all her defences, reduced her love for him to his own scale. She flung back her head

179

desperately, smoothing the tumbled silvery strands.

"Physical attraction at its lowest level!" she said bitterly, hearing in her head Lorna Talbot's scathing tones.

She was hardly prepared for his flare of violent reprisal. He jerked her to him, lavishing no consideration on her delicate collarbone.

"You're lucky I don't slap you for that one! I'll just have to allow that you're either mad or you've allowed yourself to be grossly misled!"

"That's fine talking!" she said wildly, tortured by something inexplicable in his face. He almost flung her from him, his eyes so coldly brilliant she would have welcomed the relief of hell fire.

"Enjoy your freedom!" he said cuttingly. "You want everything and you give nothing, but thank you for teaching me how to see reason!" He gave a wry laugh. "Did that sting? Small wonder! I'm afraid it was meant to. I've discovered at last that you're no more than a reckless little idiot, impulsive by nature!"

"Gray!" Her eyes were too big for her face, her voice wounded.

"Save it!" he flashed out with fine scorn. "Next thing you'll tell me I led you on, and you too innocent for my worldly ways. Let's call it quits, Perri. A pity nothing could come of it, but you're quite impossible! You deserve to make a mess of your life, but not mine!"

And that was the final insult! Perri stared at the ground, fighting the tears of hurt and humiliation, more vulnerable than she had ever been, almost morbidly sensitive. It was impossible to talk to that straight, inflexible back, the wide, powerful shoulders. Then he was gone, back down the staircase and out of the house. She was chilled to the bone, struck by lightning. She sank down on to the tapestry chair, trembling all over, almost wishing for an early death.

Would she never forget that episode? He was impossible to fathom. Or could she in her stupidity have misread the whole situation? She felt young and desperately hurt, bewildered, sick! Surely love didn't last a lifetime? If it did, she was doomed from the start. No warmth and happiness anywhere!

CHAPTER VIII

THE distant hills to the west were sharply outlined against the peacock sky, the bush and the grasslands resounding to the calls of the birds, the rose-pink galahs and the shrieking sulphur-crested cockatoos, the thousands of tiny green budgerigars that swooped low all over the flats. Perri was about three miles out from the homestead, riding south-west, allowing Mirri, her gentle little mare, to walk along the edge of the damp sands of an ovate-shaped pool, beautiful beyond belief. There were a myriad greens, almond to emerald, overhung with flowering bauhinias, pink and cerise blossoms floating on its still surface. The reeds around the pool formed a wide semi-circle which moved faintly in a spirit dance. Gray had once told them the pool was associated with an ancient myth hero, and her uncle had recorded the legend. In a seemingly vast and empty land, every step was paved with some lovely Dreamtime legend. Even now, after two short months in the Outback, she could scarcely bear to disengage herself from it. It was a world of live magic, with witch doctors and sorcerers and corroborees around the sacred fires.

She walked the little mare through the bauhinias and feathery acacias until she came out on the grass flats. A heavy rainstorm had fallen a few days before and the broad valleys of cane grass were adrift with tawny gold wild flowers, their faces turned up like fairy folk. Above her a falcon coasted, its wings slanting in the wind, making a swirling pattern in the light south-westerly, and she watched it with a hand upraised to shield her eyes. Dead ahead, a silver-boled ghost gum, the Shining One, drew her like a magnet, its base decorated in ochres of red and white and yellow. It was a spirit tree as the marks indicated, a holy symbol of a powerful, unseen god. Perri reined in to the silver-spattered shade where the little chestnut mare was willing enough to pause a while, deriving some inexplicable comfort from the aura of the revered spot, not realising she had a rare susceptibility to psychic impressions. The memory of her days on Coorain would never dim, always to remain with her, a message of peace and great freedom, of a great heritage; a brown people and an ancient civilisation. The aborigines had been deprived of their old hunting grounds, but the still, melancholy aura of their sacred places and altars pervaded the land.

At the end of the flat, which ran into the hill country, Perri saw a faint plume of smoke. She blinked her eyes. In the thin, dry air it was easy to see unreal things. No, it *was* smoke and not the leaping mirage. Perhaps a little "thank you" fire, small leafy twigs of the bush willow burnt in honour of some benevolent spirit. She rode towards it to investigate, the flush of golden light falling over her in heat waves.

183

An emu suddenly strode out of a clump of napunyah trees, its tail plumes dipping, then just as she turned to look at it, it raced away at the sight of her and Mirri treading the sea of mirage. Nearing the rocky outcrop, Perri felt a growing presentiment come on her, a strange excess of anxiety, unease of body and mind. The moan reached her and she felt herself caught and held by its crucial quality. She dismounted and securely tethered the mare to an acacia, then walked on a hundred yards, calling, no mean achievement because she was almost faint with nameless dreads, the impulse towards flight strong. But the moan in this almost limitless land made her hasten.

She picked her way around the rocky cairn with exaggerated care, then a bell rang in her head as she approached it from the other side. She was on sacred ceremonial ground, the rock pool, where time began. The glittering surface of the water struck at her eyesight, the pure white sand marred by a stone gargoyle ... Inkarta, a dark figure lying in the stark distorted position of anguish.

She drew close to him without sign of fear. She alone would have to deal with him. There was nobody else, and for all his frightening appearance he was barely clinging to life. Saliva dripped from his mouth and he waved a black, emaciated arm at her, the whites of his eyes showing, then abruptly he seemed to collapse, the little fire of twigs not far from his head.

He could have been dead! Without any apparent shift in wind, *wulpirras*, little dust spouts, rose from the sand until the whole rock shelter seemed alive with their flittings. Perhaps she had angered the spirits who guarded the place.

She crouched down on her knees beside the old medicine man and gazed at him almost fearfully. Out of the corner of his mouth came another moan that made her flesh creep. There was no doubt he was dying. One needed little experience to read the signs. Perri hurried back to the mare and found a rug and the water canteen. She returned to the white sands, slipping the folded rug under the old witch doctor's head, holding the canteen of water to his cracked, parched mouth. A little seemed to run down his throat, but most fell in great glistening drops back on to his chin and chest.

For almost an hour she sat with him while his life raced away, knowing with great certainty that even if help did reach them Inkarta stood not a chance. Once or twice he opened his eyes and looked at her; gleaming pale gold hair, white skin, and light eyes, then his milky gaze dwindled to nothing beneath his jutting brows. It might have been her imagination, but the black, impassive face seemed emptied of enmity, emptied of pain as though he had passed far beyond both. They were simply two human beings, black and white, united in a common fundamental crisis.

The sun beat down like molten gold, catching the exposed nape of her neck. She had taken off her wide-brimmed cream hat and held it across the old man's face, shielding it from the fires of the sun. Inkarta opened his eyes and looked at her. A few guttural words emerged as if he was pronouncing a sentence, but Perri saw no shade of menace in it. Gradually sounds impinged on the ruffled air; a horse running in free gallop. She rose swiftly to her feet and went back along the rocky ledge in time to see Gray swing down from the saddle, as vital and fiercely elemental as any legend. The wind swirled her hair about and he raced up the slope, gripping her arms in a storm of violence.

"I've been half out of my mind! Where in hell have you been?" His face was taut, his eyes blazing.

She clung to his hand. "But how did you find me?"

"A sheer fluke!" His voice was thin with curbed anger. "It was that wisp of smoke that attracted my attention. You can count yourself lucky I followed it. Every damn thing in the world has gone haywire. The gins in the camp have gone wild, wailing like banshees in frenzied abandon. *You* go off! I don't know what's happening on my own property!"

"It's Inkarta!" she said simply. "He's here. He's dying."

His eyes went diamond hard, a pallor under his copper-bronze skin. "You've been here with him?"

"He's dying, Gray!" she repeated. "Just an old man dying. His spirit folk around him, waiting for him to join them."

He watched her with a strange expression, his mind struggling with some element that eluded her. Then his hand descended, gripping her shoulder, guiding her back along the rock face.

One glance at the prone, corpselike figure was enough. "God!" he said, sucking in his breath. With a calm he did not feel he dropped to his knees beside the old *kur-*

daitcha man, his eyes filled with pity and the enormity of death.

"No chance at all!" he said briefly, with all the inevitability in the world compressed into those few short words. Inkarta tried to raise his head, recognising the white man, failed and sank back into a final coma, the life force failing.

It was one o'clock.

At two o'clock Inkarta died, experiencing no apparent difficulty at abandoning life, his sightless eyes looking steadily at the Sky Country. Nothing moved – not a leaf, not a bird. The wulpirras had sunk to the ground. Gray closed the old man's eyes and turned to Perri. She was leaning forward on her knees, the tears sliding unnoticed and unchecked down her sun-flushed cheeks.

"There's no need to cry!" he said in a hard, clipped voice. "The old fellow has crossed the bridge of the spirit. He's in the Sky World now, the Eternal Dreaming. All aborigines believe in the indestructibility of the human spirit. Earthly existence for them is only a brief span in the scheme of things. Come, little one, we'll go home now. Inkarta's people will come for him, long lines of them in grave procession. They know where he is from the spirit fire. The women will tell you the exact moment of his death."

He stood up and lifted her to her feet, but somehow she found herself swaying. His arms closed about her in hard possession and he swung her off her feet as if she were no more than a child and she submitted without a word. Then he turned and began to walk down the slope to the plain. In the green shade of the kurrajongs, he laid

187

her down, then sat beside her, a shadow on his dark, unyielding profile, his blue eyes on the scorching heat haze. The clear notes of a butcher bird suddenly floated down to them, sweet and pure like a benediction. The two horses stood quietly, the little mare and the splendid stallion, then arched their necks and pricked their ears as mourning chants, one after the other, rose on the wind and the spirit drums spoke across long distances.

"Do you think you could ever live here?" He turned to look down at her with all his old arrogance, no trace of emotion, as though it scarcely mattered to him what she answered.

Her eyes were huge and distressed, a sick longing playing havoc with her heart.

"I love you," she said sombrely into the hot silence, beyond pretence, driven by a compulsion she couldn't resist. "Nothing will change that. Nothing you do or I do. Whatever the pain!"

His eyes flashed, the colour of the desert sky. She could feel his swift intake of breath as if a whip had flicked him. Even the wild flowers hung motionless on their stalks, then he bent his head, with only the fleeting glimpse of his eyes to give her all the answer she craved. She breathed a little broken endearment, her hands locking behind his head, with only one will, one desire, one way possible, a wild sweet music moving through her head.

When he released her his eyes glittered and his mouth curved with love and possession. He had never seemed more vibrantly alive, the dappled sunlight on the fine concave lines of his cheek and temple.

"There are so many things I have to learn about you," he said, smoothing back the silk of her hair. "But I'll never fight out of this silver mesh you've thrown over me!"

"What *is* it you want, Gray?" she asked, studying his face with passionate hope and intensity.

"*You!*" he said with extreme persuasion, his eyes brilliant beneath his dark, slanting brows. "All the days of my life, the soft purple nights. Do you mind?"

As simply as though there were no other course of action she linked her creamy arms behind his head.

"It won't be easy for you," she told him. "I'm the one who has so much to learn. I'm lost in this great Outback, though I love it!"

"You have me!" he pointed out with all the old arrogant charm. "Together we can overcome anything!"

Under his caressing hands she scarcely knew how to broach the subject of Lorna Talbot and her daughter, but he touched her cheek, his mouth not smiling. "There will be a few necessary changes on Coorain, because that's the way it has to be. Life moves on and the whole pattern alters. You, as my wife, will come first in everything. In that respect, Lorna has always viewed an uncertain future. Never financially, I'll see to that!"

"And Kim?" she asked beneath her breath.

He tapped her cheek hard, knowing her better than she knew herself. "I heard that very clearly, and don't talk nonsense. I have never in my life had one romantic notion about Kim, and she knows it. There's no need to worry about Kim. She's young and attractive and extremely competent. She has her own future to make.

There's only one slip of a thing I can't face life without, so please leave all the little difficulties to me. I'm adept at overcoming them. In fact, I don't anticipate one unpleasant moment. Lorna has her own pride, though she's persisted over-long in her maternal fantasies. We'll arrive at a workable solution. The truth is, nothing would have much meaning for me without you. I can afford to overlook the fact that you're a strange and rather exotic young creature, an endearing mixture of fears and a screwed-up feminine courage!"

Perri looked back at him with grave dignity, but saw the teasing light in his eyes. His arms closed about her, shutting out the sun, and she gave herself up to his mood of exultant contentment, helpless to deny her own aching need.

He was Gray Faulkner, a man magnetic in his own personality, demanding, loving, tender and impatient at once, holding her in his two sure hands.

Above them the sky arched in a great cloudless vault, and the land ran away in boundless promise. The ancient land that spoke to all those who knew and loved her.

Why the smile?

. . because she has just received her **Free Harlequin Romance Catalogue!**

. . and now she has a complete listing of the many, many Harlequin Romances all available.

. . and now she can pick out titles by her favorite authors or fill in missing numbers for her library.

You too may have a **Free Harlequin Romance Catalogue** (and a smile!), simply by mailing in the coupon below.

To: HARLEQUIN READER SERVICE, Dept. N 409
M.P.O. Box 707, Niagara Falls, N.Y. 14302
Canadian address: Stratford, Ont., Canada

☐ Please send me the free Harlequin Romance Catalogue.

☐ Please send me the titles checked on following page.

I enclose $_____ (No C.O.D.'s), All books are 60c each.
To help defray postage and handling cost, please add 25c.

Name _____

Address _____

State/Prov. _____ Zip _____

BP
572

Have You Missed Any of These
Harlequin Romances?

- [ ] 812 FACTORY NURSE Hilary Neal
- [ ] 825 MAKE UP YOUR MIND NURSE
  Phyllis Matthewman
- [ ] 841 TRUANT HEART
  Patricia Fenwick
  (Original Harlequin title
  "Doctor in Brazil")
- [ ] 844 MEET ME AGAIN
  Mary Burchell
  (Original Harlequin title
  "Nurse Alison's Trust")
- [ ] 856 TOO YOUNG TO MARRY
  Rosalind Brett
- [ ] 858 MY SURGEON NEIGHBOUR
  Jane Arbor
- [ ] 873 NURSE JULIE OF WARD
  THREE   Joan Callender
- [ ] 878 THIS KIND OF LOVE
  Kathryn Blair
- [ ] 890 TWO SISTERS
  Valerie K. Nelson
- [ ] 897 NURSE HILARY'S HOLIDAY
  TASK, Jan Haye
- [ ] 898 MY DREAM IS YOURS
  Nan Asquith
  (Original Harlequin title
  "Doctor Robert Comes
  Around")
- [ ] 1074 NEW SURGEON AT ST.
  LUCIAN'S, Elizabeth
  Houghton
- [ ] 1076 BELLS IN THE WIND
  Kate Starr
- [ ] 1078 ROYAL PURPLE, Susan Barrie
- [ ] 1091 CUCKOO IN THE NIGHT
  Pamela Kent
- [ ] 1098 THE UNCHARTED OCEAN
  Margaret Malcolm
- [ ] 1109 THE FORTUNES OF SPRING-
  FIELD, Eleanor Farnes
- [ ] 1113 BEQUEST FOR NURSE
  BARBARA, Pauline Ash
- [ ] 1115 THE ROMANTIC HEART
  Norrey Ford
- [ ] 1116 PLAY THE TUNE SOFTLY
  Amanda Doyle
- [ ] 1117 DEARLY BELOVED
  Mary Burchell
- [ ] 1118 LAMENT FOR LOVE
  Jean S. Macleod

- [ ] 1121 TEAM DOCTOR, Ann Gilmour
- [ ] 1137 DOCTOR AT DRUMLOCHAN
  Iris Danbury
- [ ] 1182 GOLDEN APPLE ISLAND
  Jane Arbor
- [ ] 1183 NEVER CALL IT LOVING
  Marjorie Lewty
- [ ] 1184 THE HOUSE OF OLIVER
  Jean S. MacLeod
- [ ] 1201 THE ROMANTIC DR. RYDON
  Anne Durham
- [ ] 1209 THE STUBBORN DR.
  STEPHEN
  Elizabeth Houghton
- [ ] 1211 BRIDE OF KYLSAIG
  Iris Danbury
- [ ] 1244 WHEN LOVE IS BLIND
  Mary Burchell
- [ ] 1246 THE CONSTANT HEART
  Eleanor Farnes
- [ ] 1248 WHERE LOVE IS
  Norrey Ford
- [ ] 1253 DREAM COME TRUE
  Patricia Fenwick
- [ ] 1633 RED GINGER BLOSSOM
  Joyce Dingwell
- [ ] 1636 FLUTTER OF WHITE WINGS
  Elizabeth Ashton
- [ ] 1721 THE FLAMBOYANT TREE
  Isobel Chace
- [ ] 1722 FOLLOW A STRANGER
  Charlotte Lamb
- [ ] 1724 WEDDING AT BLUE RIVER
  Dorothy Quentin
- [ ] 1725 THE EXTRAORDINARY EN-
  GAGEMENT   Marjorie Lewty
- [ ] 1726 MAN IN CHARGE, Lilian Peake
- [ ] 1727 STRANGE BEWILDERMENT
  Katrina Britt
- [ ] 1750 THE HOUSE OF THE
  SCISSORS, Isobel Chace
- [ ] 1751 CARNIVAL COAST
  Charlotte Lamb
- [ ] 1752 MIRANDA'S MARRIAGE
  Margery Hilton
- [ ] 1753 TIME MAY CHANGE
  Nan Asquith
- [ ] 1754 THE PRETTY WITCH
  Lucy Gillen
- [ ] 1755 SCHOOL MY HEART
  Penelope Walsh
- [ ] 1756 AN APPLE IN EDEN
  Kay Thorpe

All books are 60c. Please use the handy order coupon.

M